CAN'T FIGHT THIS FEELING

KIRSTEN S. BLACKETER

DEDICATION

For those like Grace, who couldn't stand up.

For those like Marcy, who fought back and won.

For those guys like Rob, who protect and support
those they love.

TABLE OF CONTENTS

Dear Reader,

Thank you for joining me on this rad trip back to the 80s. I appreciate your love and support.

Allow me to preface this book with a few caveats. If you don't want spoilers of any kind and have no issues with unsettling content, don't read any further. I have another letter for you at the end of the story.

If you need some content forewarnings, here you go.

This book contains depictions of domestic abuse. There are scenes recalling past abuse and trauma as well as present physical and emotional abuse. While it's handled in a delicate manner, I want to give you the warning ahead of time in case this is something you wish to avoid reading for your own mental well-being.

There are also scenes that depict a character in the hospital with life-threatening injuries and death of a secondary character. This causes trauma for the main character who is an ER physician.

That being said, I understand if you choose to skip this story, but I promise I tried to address the trauma of abuse in the most tasteful way I could while bringing light to the severity of its impact on mental health and relationships. Light triumphs over darkness in the end.

Thank you for reading, and I wish you all the best.

Sincerely,
Kirsten S. Blacketer

CHAPTER ONE
MARCY

Manhattan, NYC 1985

I hate weddings.

That's the first thought I had when my brother told me he was getting married. I love Arthur and Kate, but the thought of helping to plan a wedding and being an active participant in the whole event leaves my skin crawling.

I tried it once, the whole marriage thing. It's bogus. I'd rather use my toothbrush to clean the bathrooms in Grand Central than tie the knot again.

But this isn't about what I want. This is about my brother finding the love of his life across time itself. I don't know how much of Kate's story I believe. I mean, it's pretty hard to swallow the yarn she told me.

From the future? Yeah, sure. Whatever.

But she makes my brother happy, and she's pretty awesome. So I'm not going to rain on their parade.

I slide a tip into the caterer's hand. "Thanks."

"Enjoy your party." He nods and leaves with his crew in tow.

"Did you finish those favors yet?" I ask my assistant, Liana, while I inspect the cake.

"Yeah. When did Arthur say Kate would be back?"

"Rob should be bringing her any minute." I glance at the clock. Five to five.

Arthur suggested I throw a small bachelorette party for Kate instead of a bridal shower. I had no idea what it was until he explained. I guess it's a big deal in the future. I don't know. But it gives me an excuse to kick back and relax. Work has been crazy lately, and I'm in desperate need of some downtime.

Besides, Kate doesn't have a lot of friends. And that resonates deep. I remember a time when I had no one but Arthur looking out for me. Well, Rob was there too, in a way offering support, especially that night…

I shake my head at the direction of my thoughts. I will not think about that night or my brother's best friend. Not now. Not ever.

We put the finishing touches on the decorations. The moment the door opens, Liana pops the champagne.

Kate jumps and laughs, her eyes wide as she enters Arthur's penthouse. "Marcy." She puts her hands on her hips. "Did your brother put you up to this?"

I wrap my arm around her waist and lead her into the living room I converted into our party oasis. "He may have mentioned it in passing."

"Thank you." Kate takes a champagne flute from Liana.

"You've given us a reason to celebrate." I wink and take the offered glass from Donna. "I never thought I'd see Arthur delirious in love."

"To love then." Kate lifts her glass. The small group of women around us cheer in agreement and drink.

I can't toast to that. I won't. Love ruined me. My hand trembles as I bring the glass to my lips.

A shadow flickers by the door.

Rob stands in the entryway, leaning against the doorframe, his blue eyes narrowed on me. His dark blond hair is short enough to keep it out of his eyes but long enough to run fingers through it. From a distance, he's the perfect image of a medical professional. But I've seen him up close and personal.

That man is a hazard to my health.

While Kate is distracted by the small buffet and animated conversation, I cross the room, bracing for an oncoming storm with Rob.

"Thanks for bringing Kate." I gesture to the door. "You can go now."

A lopsided smile transforms his face from serious to

amused, and he presses his hand to his heart. "That eager to kick me out? I'm hurt."

"You're so dramatic. Don't you have somewhere to be?"

"Arthur hasn't even left work." He straightens, and I'm reminded of the staggering height difference between us. He looks down at me. "Why do you hate me, Marcy?"

"I don't hate you." A lump lodges in my throat and I swallow it. "I just don't have time for playboys."

Rob scoffs. "I'm not a playboy."

"Whatever. Now shoo. This party doesn't include you." I press my hand against his chest, urging him back toward the door. He's like a brick wall beneath my hand. I ignore the way his body flexes beneath my touch.

"Fine. We'll be at the bar, then crash at my place." He collides with the wall by the door and rests his hand on the knob. "Enjoy your evening."

The moment the door closes behind him, relief and regret simultaneously slam into me. Why does he make me feel this way—twisted up and confused to the point I can't think clearly? I know there's sexual tension between us, but exploring it is not an option. Period.

I return to the party. The half dozen ladies I've gathered to celebrate Kate's status as bride-to-be are ready for food and booze. By the time we cut the cake, the tension between Rob and me has lessened to a nagging pinprick in the back of my mind.

Kate curls up on the couch beside me, balancing her plate in one hand and stabbing bits of cake with a fork. "Thanks for the party, Marcy. You didn't have to do this."

I wave my hand. "Don't worry about it. I like the idea of this much more than a stuffy, boring bridal shower."

"The only thing missing is some strippers." Kate laughs and stuffs a bite of cake in her mouth.

"Strippers?" I gawk at her before chuckling. "Why didn't I think of that?" My voice drops low so only she can hear me. "Is that a big thing in the future?"

She nods adamantly.

"The future sounds like a wild trip."

Kate's mood sobers, her eyes glistening with tears. "It's…different."

My heart goes out to her. I have no frame of reference for the emotions she must be feeling—torn from her life and thrown into the past. It must be terrifying and heartbreaking. She doesn't offer any details, but she doesn't have to. Arthur's told me enough to know she felt like an outsider in her own time.

I wrap my arm around her and pull her against me. She leans her head on my shoulder. We've all felt that way at some point, and even though she can't talk about it, I want her to know I'm here if she needs me.

"So what's going on with you and Rob?"

Well, that shatters the heartwarming moment. Kate sits up, her gaze curious when it fixes on me.

"Nothing. Why?" I sip my drink and focus on a streamer hanging on the far wall.

"Come on. I may have been here less than six months, but I'm not blind. You two have some kind of *thing* going on."

"We most certainly do not have a *thing*," I growl. "He's my brother's best friend. That's it."

"Really?" She looks unconvinced.

"Look, it's simple. The only thing we have in common is Arthur. That's it. There is nothing between us."

"Would you want something?"

"With Rob?" I scoff. "Not in a million years."

"Why?" Kate's question is like a blade through my heart. "He's a nice guy. I think you two would make a great couple."

"I just don't look at him that way."

"Why not? He looks at you like he wants to—"

"It's complicated," I snap.

Hurt fills her eyes at my harsh response.

I sigh and take her hand. "Let's not talk about this non-existent thing between Rob and me."

"I just want to see you as happy as Arthur and me." She squeezes my hand. "You deserve to be happy, Marcy."

She knows the truth of my messy past; she's just too kind

to bring it up. I'm sure Arthur has filled her in on the details of my failed marriage and my subsequent struggle. How I refused to take his money and clawed my way up from the ground to reach this point. Arthur walked beside me the whole way, but I wouldn't let him help me.

It was something I had to do myself. To prove I am strong enough to overcome what that bastard did to me.

"Thanks, sugar." I kiss her cheek. "Let's focus on you for now. In a week, you'll be married and off on your honeymoon."

"It's so exciting." Joy fills her eyes at the reminder.

"Have you picked a destination yet?"

"Italy. He's promised to show me Rome, Venice, Florence, and Milan. A whirlwind tour of the country over two weeks."

Jealousy rears its head. Not over the trip to Italy. I could buy a ticket and spend a year roaming the country with the funds I have tucked away. No, it's not the destination causing me pain; it's that she'll have Arthur by her side for the adventure. They'll share the experience, and it'll be a memory they carry into their golden years together. I can't help but envy that.

"Nona would be so proud." I beam at her, swallowing the sting of my own disappointment. "Be sure to take plenty of pictures."

"I wish I had my iPhone. This film stuff is so old-school." Kate claps her hand over her mouth. "Forget I said that."

"Oh, honey, if I don't recognize something you say, I block it out." I wink. "At some point, I'll figure it all out, but I don't need to know the future. The present is enough of a challenge."

"That's true." Kate leans back against the couch. "If there's no stripper, then what do you have planned for us?"

"Well, I have two options. Games or gossip," I tell the group as the guests gather around us. "What'll it be?"

"You work with the hottest celebrities on a daily basis," Kate's coworker, Gladys, says with a glint in her eyes. "Let's gossip."

"What about both?" Kate asks, sitting up. "Marcy can name a celebrity, and we'll ask her yes-or-no questions. If it's yes, she drinks. If it's no, we drink."

"Sounds like a dangerous game but I'm in." Liana settles a chair nearby and fills her wine glass.

While the other women scramble to fill their glasses, I prepare myself mentally for this game. Normally, I wouldn't encourage gossip about my clients. But these ladies know me well enough to keep it within the bounds of my established rules. I may work in an industry that allows me to rub shoulders with the elite of New York City, but I'm certainly not a snitch or a sellout.

"Here is the only rule." My gaze skims over the five guests and the bride-to-be. "I reserve the right to not answer a question if it crosses the line of client confidentiality, but I'll entertain all questions before making that decision. Deal?"

"Deal," they chime in unison.

"All right, Kate. You pick the first celebrity."

"Jon Bon Jovi." Her eyes sparkle. "Is his hair as soft as it looks?"

With a wicked grin, I salute her and take a drink. The ladies cheer my confirmation.

The evening continues with laughter and scandalous revelations about our favorite celebrities. Since I found success as a stylist to the stars, my view of celebrity culture has changed. I see them as people first, not commodities. Not all of them are pleasant, but for every asshole, there are ten who treat me with respect and courtesy.

I've spent a lot of time building my reputation as the top stylist in the city. It doesn't put me in the spotlight like being an actor would, but it's my passion and I'm proud of my accomplishments.

By the end of the night, I'm pleasantly exhausted. I'm not as young as my mind thinks I am, and these late nights take their toll. I'm closing in on forty. That alone terrifies me. The last thing I want is to wake up at seventy with regrets. Maybe I should start figuring out what I want to do outside of my established empire.

In one week, my brother will be married to a wonderful woman, and I'll be on my own again.

That's not true. My family will expand with Kate's presence.

I just can't help but feel the gaping hole in my chest expanding.

Why should I need a man? I've done just fine without one. The last thing I need is another asshole barging into my life, ruining my hard work, and stealing my thunder before beating me unconscious.

To hell with marriage and men.

After Arthur and Kate's wedding next week, I'll wash my hands of the whole institution.

CHAPTER TWO
ROB

There isn't a woman alive who gets under my skin like Marcy Maxwell.

The warm spring air intensifies the heat simmering in my veins. As I make my way across town, my mind wars with my body.

How can one woman be both the bane of my existence and the object of all my fantasies?

I grab the subway heading toward Hell's Kitchen. It's a lovely day, and I should take the opportunity to walk through Central Park. It would burn off this thrumming need threatening to tear me apart. But I promised I'd meet Arthur at six.

It's already twenty after five. Shit.

After fighting the work rush, I manage to find a spot on the subway. The crush of people does nothing to quell the heat. It's going to be a hot summer if this is any indicator. Heat inevitably leads to more work for me.

Arthur has told me countless times to give up the grind of the emergency room and start my own practice. But I can't. There's something about triage medicine—the rush of adrenaline in saving someone's life—that brings my purpose on this rock into focus.

Granted, Arthur uses me as his own personal physician 90 percent of the time. Like the whole fiasco with him knocking Kate unconscious and refusing to take her to the hospital. In that specific case, I understood. Her situation was unique. I wouldn't have wanted to explain it to the boss. Sometimes, bureaucracy gets in the way. I won't turn down help for someone who needs it, regardless of whether they're in my ER or on the street.

The subway reaches my stop, and I make my way out of the

station, desperate for some fresh air. Sunny blue skies stretch overhead, but I'm focused on weaving through the crowded sidewalks.

Today's the first day I've had off in two weeks. I took Kate to finalize a few last-minute wedding arrangements at Arthur's request, and Marcy wanted to surprise her with a bachelorette party, whatever the hell that is. I thought women were supposed to have bridal showers? Not that it matters. Any excuse to see Marcy is worth it.

By the time I reach the Black Penny, it's after six. There's a decent gathering already. The dockhands often stop to grab a drink before heading home.

Claude appears when I slide onto a bench at the bar. He's already pouring gin over ice with his one hand. "The usual, Rob?"

"Yeah." I admire his ability to navigate the bar with one arm. Well, one hand really. We've been coming to the Black Penny for years. Claude took it over from his grandfather after he came back from Vietnam. Amputation of the left proximal radial and ulna can take a toll on anyone. But he's adapted. He never talks about it or his time in Vietnam. We never ask, although it does pique my medical curiosity.

He places my gin and tonic on a napkin and slides it toward me. I place a twenty on the bar. "I'm paying tonight, got it? Don't let Arthur tell you otherwise."

"No problem." Claude's gaze flickers to a spot over my shoulder as his hand closes around the bill.

"Don't let me do what?" Arthur materializes behind me.

I jump and press a hand to my heart. "Fuck, Arthur, why do you have to sneak up on me like that?"

"I didn't sneak up on you. You're distracted." He takes the stool next to mine. "Scotch, neat."

Claude's already placed the drink in front of him. "Just flag me down when you need a refill." He crosses to the opposite end of the bar.

"Kate surprised at her party?" Arthur lifts the drink and inhales deeply before indulging.

"Yeah." I chuckle at the memory of Kate's expression, but it's immediately replaced by a vision of Marcy's fury. "Your sister did good."

"Glad to hear it." He sets the glass down.

"Your sister hates me." The words spill from my mouth. I'd blame the gin, but I've barely ingested any.

"She doesn't hate you." Arthur glances at me, his eyes dark. "She doesn't like men in general. Can you blame her?"

"No. But after twenty years, you'd think she'd warm up to me." I scoff. "It'd be nice not to have my head bitten off every time I try to talk to her. I'm not like her asshole ex."

"I know." He claps his hand on my shoulder. "Don't take it personally."

"I don't." Yes, I do. Every fucking time. It's exhausting.

"Good."

Several tense moments pass, and I wash thoughts of Marcy down with my gin. Claude returns with a bowl of pretzels. I grab one and nibble on it. I should order something to eat, but my stomach is twisted in knots.

"Are you ready for the wedding?" I watch Arthur's profile.

"Ready as I'll ever be. I never imagined I would get married." He shakes his head and laughs. "Especially not to a girl from the future."

"Yeah, I still have a hard time figuring out the logistics of that." I chuckle. "But she's good for you. I'm glad you found someone who'll deal with your grumpy ass."

Arthur straightens. "I'm not grumpy."

"Whatever you say."

"I'm not."

Claude reappears, and I seize the opportunity. "Claude, is Arthur grumpy?"

The bartender's expression remains neutral as his gaze drifts between us. "Don't drag me into this. I'm here to serve drinks, not mediate your petty bullshit."

I frown. "You're no fun."

Claude shrugs and retreats to the far end of the bar.

"He knows us too well." Arthur smirks before finishing the

last of his scotch. "I booked the flight to Rome. We leave the day after the wedding."

"I'm jealous, man. I've always wanted to see Italy."

"So go. Nothing's stopping you."

"That's not the point. You have someone to share it with."

Arthur sighs and pivots to face me. "So find someone and go."

"You say that like it's the easiest thing in the world."

"If you'd stop mooning over my sister, you'd find someone."

I choke on my gin. "I'm not mooning over Marcy."

"Yes, you are. You have been for years. It's fucking exhausting—you two go back and forth like two stray cats. Admit it, she's not interested. You should move on."

But I don't want to. The words echo in my mind. I finish the gin and slide the glass away. "Point taken."

"Oh, speaking of my sister, she'll be staying at the penthouse while we're away. Kate insisted on getting a cat, and Marcy offered to keep an eye on her." He pauses, tapping the glass on the bar. "I told her to call you if she has any issues."

"Thanks. That'll help me move on." I groan and rest my head on the table.

"You're welcome."

Claude appears and refills our glasses. The conversation shifts to more neutral topics, mostly work and snatches of gossip about our mutual friends. I enjoy spending time with Arthur when he's not breaking my balls. But I can hand it right back to him.

Right now, though, I don't. He's getting married, and we're celebrating. I'm happy for him and Kate. They deserve each other. I couldn't have envisioned a better match.

The longer we sit at the bar, the more we drink. Claude cuts us off at ten o'clock and starts pushing water in our direction. By the time midnight rolls around, we're drunk and carefree, but not completely wasted.

Claude kicks us out shortly after midnight.

A black town car appears, and Cyril steps from the driver's

seat. He opens the back door, and with a disapproving shake of his head over our state of intoxication, he nudges us into the car.

Thirty minutes later, we arrive at our building. Arthur lives in the penthouse, and I'm in one of the smaller apartments several floors below. It's convenient, living near my best friend. But it's also a curse.

As we enter the building, we pass a gaggle of women. Arthur returns to Cyril for a hushed conversation as I stand with the door open, like a gentleman.

Then I see her. Marcy. The only woman in this world who I crave. Her eyes flash bright beneath the streetlight overhead, and her lips purse when she sees me. The rest of the women pass by, leaving me to face her alone.

"I trust you had a lovely evening?"

Marcy faces me. "It was illuminating."

"What does one do at a bachelorette party?" I muse, my voice swaying from the effects of the gin.

"Drink. Gossip. Play games. Watch men strip and throw money at them."

"What?" My eyes widen. Surely I misheard her.

"Looks like indulging in half-naked men before you're married is all the rage in the future."

"But why?"

"I guess girls just want to have fun." She brushes past me.

"Marcy…" My voice trails off when she stops and turns.

She props her hand on her hip, and the neon glow of her top catches the streetlight, making her shine.

"What, Rob?" She snaps her gum.

"Nothing." I shake my head. "Sleep well."

With a scoff, she walks away. Arthur helps her into the car along with the other women. Cyril casts a pleading look my way before rounding the car and getting in the driver's seat.

"You're having him drive them home?" I ask Arthur when he joins me.

"Of course. I pay him well enough. He'll be fine."

I follow Arthur to the elevator and press the button for my floor. He presses his. Silence descends in the car as it rises.

"Thanks for tonight," Arthur says as the elevator comes to a stop on my floor.

"Of course." I exit and turn, saluting him. "Go home to your wife."

A smile tugs at his lips. "With pleasure."

The doors slide closed.

When I open my apartment, the soft glow of the lamp next to the sofa lights the room. It's small but tidy. I don't spend all of my money on a lavish place. I rarely sleep here. It fits my needs.

With a groan, I head for the shower. I let the warm spray soothe me as I lean against the wall. Thoughts of Marcy flood my brain. Why does she plague me? I'd give anything to purge her from my soul, to find someone who actually likes me…wants me.

My cock hardens at the memory of her pink lips and her glow under the streetlight. I take it in my hand and stroke until I'm consumed by nothing but her, by the pleasure lying just out of reach. Panting breaths echo off the tiles. When I come, I imagine her face. Her body. Marcy.

Fuck. I'm a goddamn lost cause.

After drying off and brushing my teeth, I collapse in bed, then stare at the ceiling. I have to work at eight a.m., but sleep eludes me. I'm wrapped up in her. I can't keep fighting this pull.

But how can I convince someone of something when they're dead set against it?

I roll to my side, and the sheet slides low on my hips. Shit, how am I hard again?

Somehow, I have to convince her of the truth. I love her, and I've loved her for years. But how the fuck do I show her?

Convincing her of anything is like walking on broken glass. But I'll gladly do it if it gives me the chance to make her mine.

CHAPTER THREE
MARCY

Come Monday morning, it's business as usual. Stale cigarette smoke and expensive perfume cling to the air when I walk into the studio. I wave to the crew as I weave through the equipment. My staff will arrive any minute with the garment racks and accessories.

The manager points me to the area they've set aside for costumes and styling. The makeup artists and hairstylists have already arrived and greet me with air-kisses. We've worked together on projects in the past. At this point in my career, I know most of the major players in the industry with roots in the city.

"How was your weekend?" I ask when my reliable employees arrive with the covered garment racks.

"Totally rad," Trixie gushes. She's a whiz when it comes to hair. "Hit a party on the Upper East Side. What about you?"

"Oh, yeah. Me too. It was an intimate get-together though. Very exclusive."

Liana catches my eye and hides a grin behind her hand. We're very selective about the information we share within the industry. Too much propensity for gossip. I like to keep my personal details under wraps, so I cultivate a persona that fits the bill. My girls know this and support it 100 percent.

"Bitchin'." Kit, the makeup artist, slides from her seat by the window and stubs out her cigarette. "Did they tell you who we're styling today?"

"A couple of new artists for an MTV slot and an actor from that show everyone's raving about."

"Vic Simmons." Trixie swoons dramatically. "He's so choice."

I snap my gum and shrug. "Never heard of him."

"Seriously?" Liana gawks at me. "You've watched that detective show he was in—"

She snaps her mouth shut at my stern look. I peel the cover off the rack and skim through the clothing selection I packed yesterday.

"Oh, that's him? Huh." I play it off while Liana positions the other racks along the wall.

"That role as the brooding detective set him up. He's hot stuff now." Kit pops her gum and fixes her hair in the mirror. She readjusts her crop top, ensuring her breasts are at their most visible. "I heard he's single. Dumped that actress he was with last month."

"Really?" Trixie perks up. "Dibs."

"You can't call dibs," Kit snaps. "All's fair in love and war, honey."

Trixie sticks out her tongue and then applies a generous gloss to her already pouty lips.

These two are ten years younger than me, and they act it. They have no idea what a steady relationship is, judging from the banter I regularly hear. Not that I hold it against them. Truth is I'm jealous. I wish I had spent my twenties having fun and hitting on every guy who crossed my path. Unfortunately, most of that decade of my life was spent hidden in a small apartment afraid I'd end up in the ER because I'd made him mad. Again.

I shake the thoughts away. No. He doesn't warrant a moment of my time. The past is gone, and I'm not going to give another man that kind of power over me. Ever.

"Isn't he in his forties?" Liana asks. "I didn't know you guys liked older men."

"It's Vic. He's hot for an old guy." Trixie tugs her pink-and-gray ripped tee shirt to the side, exposing her shoulder.

I bite my tongue. They're only after the sex and the status. They don't care about the nitty-gritty details of a relationship.

Oh, to be young and carefree again.

A knock at the door interrupts us. The stage manager pops his head inside. "Ready when you are."

"Bring them in." I nod and take charge. Trixie and Kit ready their stations while Liana and Donna organize the rest of the clothing.

Three gorgeous women enter the room. They all look vaguely familiar. But then again, everyone does in this industry. I've worked with them before, but they don't acknowledge the prior connection. They see so many stylists throughout the course of their careers. I don't take it personally when they're so distracted they forget they've met me. In this industry, we're just the magicians behind the scenes. And even though we don't get the recognition we deserve on camera, the studio knows exactly who they want working for them. After a quick greeting, we launch into action. Time to make some magic.

We rotate stations—one with hair, one with makeup, while we dress the third. It's fluid and effortless.

I live for this job. It's my only love. Style. Fashion. But most of all, I love the control. Being my own boss. No one questions my taste…not anymore. I've worked for heads of state and Hollywood's elite. Nothing surprises me at this stage of the game, and best of all, they trust my judgment when it comes to wardrobe.

When I've finished the second artist's look, the manager appears in the doorway. "Marcy, Mr. Simmons is ready for you."

Kit and Trixie glance up simultaneously to meet my gaze in the mirror.

"I'll be there in a moment." Once he disappears, I gather the garments I set aside for him and motion for Liana to join me. "Donna, finish up here." I glance at Trixie and Kit. "I'll send him over when I'm done."

Their expressions fluctuate between jealousy and disbelief. I almost make a sexual innuendo, but I refrain. I don't need gossip to spread that I've set my sights on a client. I certainly don't mix business with pleasure. No matter how tempting it might be.

Liana grabs the garments in my hand and follows as we step from the dressing room. The manager leads us to a room down the hall and leaves us.

I knock on the door. "Mr. Simmons?"

"Come in." A deep voice echoes within.

When I enter, my whole body ceases to function. Mr. Simmons is standing in only a robe, his dark hair tousled, his blue eyes sparkling, and his lips curved in a tempting grin. Shit. He's even more handsome in person than on TV.

Somehow, I manage to regain control of my brain and my limbs. "Good morning. I'm Marcy, this is Liana. I'm your stylist for the day."

"Lovely." His gaze rakes over me, and I can't stop the heat from rising in my face.

I turn and take the garments from Liana's arm. Keeping my back to him, I hang them on a hook behind the door. With a deep breath, I face him once more. My gaze lingers on his broad shoulders as I take in his form, estimating measurements.

"We'll go with the navy blue. It'll bring out his eyes, and the fit should be perfect." I gesture for Liana to prepare the suit. "Now, Mr. Simm—"

"Vic." His deep voice rumbles through me. "Call me Vic."

"If you insist." I clear my throat. "Vic, do you have an undershirt?"

He tugs the hem of the robe aside to reveal only bare skin beneath the fabric. "Never wear one."

"I see." My heart pounds in my chest and I struggle to ignore the allure of this man. "Well, in that case, we'll go with a darker shirt. I think the black will work, don't you, Liana?"

"Yes." She frowns as she skims through the bag. "It must be on the rack. I'll go get it."

"Perfect. Thank you."

Liana steps out of the room, leaving the door cracked, and the earlier tension transforms into a physical presence.

Vic patiently stands at a reasonable distance, yet I feel claustrophobic. It's not a bad feeling, but it's one I've purposely avoided for years.

"Here…" I pull the pants from the hanger and cross to where he's standing. "Put these on. I'm pretty sure they'll fit like a glove."

Vic's gaze doesn't waver as he pulls the robe off his shoulders. There's only a tempting expanse of skin dusted with hair and an intoxicating scent of his aftershave. He drapes the robe over the chair and takes the pants from me. My gaze dips to his waist. I stifle a moan at the sight of his muscular thighs and the briefs gripping his hipbones, barely containing his obvious arousal.

I avert my gaze as he draws the pants up and fixes them around his waist.

"They fit perfectly." He grins. "You've got a good eye."

"What can I say? I'm good at my job." I snap my gum.

"You certainly are."

I don't miss the glint of hunger in his eyes. Why did I send Liana for that shirt? I know better than to break my own rule—never remain alone with a client, male or female. It leaves too much room for unwanted drama. I've seen too much shit that could have been avoided if there were witnesses.

And yet here I am. Alone with a client who obviously sees something he likes.

As if summoned by my thoughts, Liana opens the door. "Found it."

"Thank you." I gesture to Vic. "If you'll give him that, I'll get the tie and jacket."

Taking a moment to regain my composure, I pull the jacket and tie off the hanger. When I turn, my mouth waters at the sight of Vic shrouded in dark colors, molded to his body like a second skin. It should be illegal for him to look that good.

I pass the jacket to Liana and hold up the tie. "Can you handle this part?"

He scoffs and grabs the silk tie from my hand. The fabric slides between my fingers, making me shiver.

My mind wanders as he loops it around his neck, beneath his collar. He works quickly, tying it in a perfect Windsor knot. All without glancing in the mirror or breaking eye contact.

"How does it look?"

"Fantastic," Liana says with awe. "You're a magician."

Vic laughs. "No. I had a lot of practice tying them on set. I didn't have gorgeous stylists to help me then."

Liana's face turns pink. She hands me the jacket. I hold it open. He turns and places his arms in the sleeves. It slides over his shoulders and settles into place, perfectly framing his body. I suppress a shiver caused by the heat building between us and step away.

"Magic." He meets my gaze. "Thank you, Marcy."

"Any time." I drop my hands to my sides. "I'll have hair and makeup come to your room in a moment."

Liana gathers the remaining items and opens the door. I'm half in the hallway when his voice stops me.

"See you around."

I meet his gaze, and my pulse flutters at the sincerity on his face. With a smile, I close the door behind me, cutting him from my view.

Liana nudges me with her elbow. "Was he flirting with you?"

"Yeah." I shrug like it doesn't matter, but inside, my body's humming. I've had clients flirt with me before. Senators, actors, musicians, talk show hosts—you name it, they've hit on me.

But it's never affected me the way Vic's flirting has. He's all charm, the way Dan used to be. It's a red flag, and I know better than to get involved with a client. That's a one-way ticket to disaster.

"Why didn't you flirt back?" she asks, keeping her voice low.

"Because I don't fool around with celebrities. And I certainly don't date clients." I pin her with a knowing look. "You've worked for me long enough to know this. I don't mix business with pleasure."

"I know." She pouts. "But he looked like he wanted to throw you over his shoulder and find the nearest bedroom."

I chuckle. "You don't need a bedroom…just a door with a lock."

"That's true."

I open the door to the main dressing room. Kit and Trixie spin around expectantly, then frown when it's only me. "Mr.

Simmons is waiting for you both in his dressing room."

"Finally." Trixie grabs her gear and heads for the door. Kit follows close behind.

I shake my head and focus on the young woman Donna is dressing in a long shimmery dress.

As we finalize her look, my mind wanders to Vic.

It's not like I haven't been interested in any men. I am. But I'm not interested in anything more than a one-night stand. That doesn't work well in this industry. And the one man I'd even consider breaking my longstanding rule for...well, he's not even an option. Vic isn't Rob. No one is.

My brother's best friend is completely off-limits. Rob deserves a woman who will give him everything he's always wanted. And I can't give him that.

I'm broken and jaded. No one wants the *real* me.

CHAPTER FOUR

ROB

It must be a full moon. The ER is crammed to full capacity. It's even busier than usual for a Friday afternoon. I've only been on the clock for four hours, and I'm already exhausted. The bustle of commotion around me leaves me in an adrenaline-induced haze.

On days like today, I'm actually thankful for the activity—keeps my mind off the rehearsal dinner tonight and my best friend's wedding tomorrow.

But it doesn't block the ever-present thoughts of Marcy. Shit.

Summer, one of the nurses on duty, rushes up to me with a chart in her hand. "Dr. Thompson, I need your assistance in exam two."

"What do we have?" I take the chart and flip through it.

"Female. Mid-twenties. Came in complaining of stabbing pain in her abdomen." She rushes on before I can ask any standard questions. "She has bruising."

I glance up from the chart. "On the abdomen?"

"Yes, but that's not where it concerns me." Summer lowers her voice. "She has a black eye and swelling on her left cheek and along the jaw."

"You asked her what happened?"

"Yes. She says she tripped over the mop bucket in the kitchen and hit the counter when she fell." Summer doesn't seem convinced by this story, and neither am I.

"Does she have anyone with her?"

"Her husband." Summer shifts her weight from one foot to the other. "He refuses to step outside so we can speak to her alone."

"Shit." I rake my fingers through my hair. "Okay. I'll take a look."

The unknown variables play in my mind as I head for the exam room, Summer following. She takes her place by my side in the curtained area. The woman on the gurney glances up. The left side of her face is swollen and purple, exactly how Summer described. She's clutching her side, just over the liver. Fuck.

The man beside her hovers, his arms folded across his chest. He doesn't look the part, but you don't have to look like a bully to beat the shit out of someone. Flashbacks to the night Marcy left her ex flood back in a rush. The bruises, the cuts, the blood. I shove the memories away and focus on the patient in front of me.

"Hello, I'm Dr. Thompson." I offer a friendly smile. The man grunts when I sit on the chair beside the bed. I ignore him and focus solely on the patient. "What's your name?"

"Grace."

"What's going on, Grace?"

"I fell. In the kitchen." The woman's voice is strong, but her hands tremble. "My side hurts. Feels like something's broken."

"Do you mind if I take a look?" I hand the chart to Summer and gesture to Grace's side.

Her gaze shifts from me to the man beside her. He nods. Fury shoots through me, but I maintain calm. I don't want to escalate this situation. Confrontation in an emergency room isn't uncommon, but it's highly disruptive. I try to avoid it if I can.

She moves her hands and I gently palpate the area. She winces at the pressure and fists her hands in the sheets. Her face pales, and she bites her lip to suppress cries of pain. Poor kid. I inspect the area thoroughly before leaning back to give her space once more.

"There's definitely something going on here. But before I make a definitive diagnosis, I'd like to get a CAT scan of the area to get a better idea of the possible damage."

"A CAT scan?" The man huffs. "Is that necessary?"

"I need to be sure there's nothing broken and her liver isn't damaged or hemorrhaging. It could just be inflammation, but I need to be sure before settling on a course of action to treat it." I turn my attention back to Grace, who looks terrified. "Do I have your permission to get a CAT scan?"

She glances at *him* again. I clench my hands into fists and take a deep breath. I want to kick his ass out of the room, but if I do, he'll surely throw a fit and lash out. No, I have to play this with finesse.

Reluctantly, the asshole nods.

Grace breathes a sigh of relief. "Yes, please, it hurts terribly."

"Don't worry, Grace. We'll give you something for the pain and have you right as rain in no time." My reassuring smile seems to ease her discomfort.

I turn to her husband. "Sir, if you'll step into the waiting room, I'm going to need you to take care of some paperwork while your wife is in having the scan done."

"She can't go alone. I have to be with her." His agitation is growing. "She needs me."

"Sir, it will only be a few moments. As soon as she's done, we'll bring you right back here," I assure him. But I wish I were lying. I have no legal recourse to keep them separated. My hands are tied for the moment.

"Fine." He steps aside as two nurses come in to wheel the gurney from the room. Summer guides the agitated husband to the front desk while I follow the patient down the hall toward radiology.

The moment we pass through the doors. Grace bursts into tears. She grips her side.

"It's okay, Grace. We'll get you fixed up in a jiffy."

She shakes her head, and the tears continue.

"Grace, I'm going to ask you some questions. I'd like you to answer them as honestly as possible."

Her wide green eyes are full of tears. She hiccups, then gives me a tiny nod.

"Good girl." I keep my voice low. "Do you feel safe at home?"

A fresh round of tears bursts forth. "I can't...I can't answer that."

"Sweetheart, if you're not safe and need an advocate, now is your chance. I'll do everything in my power to help you."

"I can't talk about it." She whimpers between sobs. "He'll…I can't." She hides her face with her hands. The force of crying makes her moan with pain.

"Shh, it'll be okay, Grace. I understand." Regret stabs me. Too many times I've been in this position, and there's not a damn thing I can do. I can't help her if she doesn't want my help. If I step in without her consent, she'll catch hell when they're alone again. It's a twisted situation, and I'm not mentally prepared for the onslaught of past emotions rising to the surface. I shove them aside and focus on my patient.

We reach radiology. I ask to the nurse wheeling the gurney to retrieve some medication from the pharmacy. The CAT scan tech appears by my side. I give him instructions and request a female tech to come on board with this particular patient. I want her to feel safe. Having that extra layer of protection isn't because I don't trust the tech. It's because she's vulnerable, and damn it, she deserves a moment of peace.

The two technicians take her into the room.

I lean against the counter at the nurse's station and take a breath. All I can do now is pray the CAT scan comes back clear. It could be broken ribs, a lacerated liver, hemorrhage, or a dozen other issues. I can't be sure of anything until I get a look at what's going on inside her. But I sure as hell know what's going on outside.

That fucker raised his hand to her. He put those bruises there. I can tell by the way she looked to him for answers to every question. She waited for his approval before agreeing to anything.

This is a classic case of domestic abuse.

And there's not a goddamn thing I can do about it. The pencil in my hand snaps in two.

I wait until the CAT scan is done and escort Grace back to the ER. There are a half dozen patients waiting for me, but I can't leave her. Not until I'm sure it's not life-threatening.

When we reach the exam room, he's waiting for us. Grace blanches at the sight of him and drops her gaze to her hands. I instruct the nurse to give her the pain meds. I ask a series of questions about her medical and family history. By the time I finish, the tech arrives with the CAT scan report. I review the results with a critical eye.

Nothing. Relief fills me. Her liver is enflamed, but there's nothing concerning on the scan. I explain this to her, and with a sigh, she relaxes against the pillow.

I give her instructions to follow and a scrip for medication to bring down the inflammation. "Now remember, if the pain persists or increases, I want you to come right back here. Okay?"

"Yes, Doctor."

My gaze drifts to her husband, whose eagle eyes are narrowed on me. I meet his glare with one of my own, one that clearly states I know exactly what he did to his wife and I will not tolerate it happening again. Telepathy doesn't work, but I think he gets the point.

The asshole shifts his weight uncomfortably. "Can we go?"

"Yes." I glance at Grace. "Take care of yourself."

"Thank you, Doctor." Her tentative smile pierces my conscience. Before I make a fool of myself, I exit the exam room.

The rest of my shift passes in a blur of activity. I don't have a chance to dwell on what happened with Grace or the horror it dredged up from my past. I couldn't protect Marcy, and I can't protect Grace. I did the best I could under the circumstances and curse my restraints.

When I finally leave the ER, I'm fucking exhausted. I want to go home and crash. But I can't.

I glance at my watch. I have just enough time to get home, shower, and run out the door again. The rehearsal dinner starts at seven. I don't want to be late. Arthur will kill me.

But I'm in no mood to be sociable. The weight of the day rests heavily on me, like a vice constricting my chest. I can't push it away. The cloud hangs over my head and threatens to unleash hell.

Goddamn it.

Seeing Marcy tonight isn't going to improve my mood.

It should. She's the one bright spot in my life, and I would give anything to spend time with her, even if she hates me. But after the incident in the ER, I'm reminded of just how close I came to losing her. Even though she was never mine to begin with.

I love Marcy. I loved her before she married that asshole. When she showed up on Arthur's doorstep with a suitcase, bleeding and broken, I patched her up. But she wouldn't let me close. I couldn't blame her. Who the fuck would want another relationship after that?

But it didn't curb my feelings for her. It intensified them.

Her resolve and determination after her divorce fed her success. She made something beautiful from the wreckage of her life. I commend her.

When I get home, I manage to throw myself together in a presentable manner and head for the restaurant. It'll be fine. I'll be fine. I'll just bury my disappointment and pain and deal with them later. Tonight is about Arthur and Kate.

The closer I get to the restaurant, the more I want to turn around and go home. I'm in a fucking mood, and I'm afraid everyone is going to see it.

Especially Marcy. And the last thing I want to do is upset her.

CHAPTER FIVE
MARCY

I don't like this—Rob and I having dinner with Kate and Arthur. It feels too much like a double date.

We're seated at a round table in one of the most prestigious restaurants in the city. The lights are low, and the instrumental music is atmospheric with a whimsical touch of romance. Sitting here watching my brother make calf eyes at the woman of his dreams is making me uncomfortable.

No, actually that part isn't bothering me nearly as much as the undeniably masculine presence to my left. Rob's somber mood radiates off him in waves as he picks at the chicken on his plate. He hasn't spoken more than six words all night. It's not like him.

Kate's outlining the itinerary for their trip to Italy. Since Rob isn't invested in the conversation, I jump in and ask questions. I'm happy for her and Arthur, but I won't lie, I'm a bit jealous of the lovely honeymoon they have planned.

"You've been to Rome, haven't you, Rob?" Kate asks, turning her attention to the brooding beast beside me.

"Once." He sets his fork aside and takes a drink of his wine. "For an international conference."

"Did you get to see any of the historic sites while you were there?" Kate's eyes flash with interest.

"Not really. I think we drove past the Colosseum, but I didn't get to look around."

"That's a shame." Kate pouts. "Arthur's promised to point out all the architectural wonders during our trip." She covers his hand with hers.

I take a drink of my wine to stop a sarcastic comment. *Be happy for them. It's not their fault you're a jaded old woman.*

"You're still able to stay at the apartment and watch the cat, right?" Arthur focuses on me.

"I…uh…well, I don't know if I'll be able to." I shift uncomfortably in my chair. "My schedule changed and I need to be at the studio early. My apartment is closer to work, so it'll save me some time if I stay at my place. Sorry."

"What about you, Rob?" Kate turns to him. "Would you be willing to stay at the penthouse while we're gone?"

"I probably won't be there much. I'm on call next week." Rob fidgets with the stem of the glass.

"Oh, that's fine. I just want to be sure Tabby's taken care of."

"I mean, I can check on the cat in the evenings, if you want," I add, sensing conflict brewing.

"No, don't go out of your way." Kate beams at Rob. "Tabby's pretty shy anyway. Just feed her twice a day, and you'll have a friend for life."

"I can handle that." Rob's relenting nod doesn't foster confidence.

I search his profile, noting the firm set of his jaw and the crow's-feet at the corners of his eyes. I recognize his body language. He's holding back. Putting on a front. It's as familiar to me as my own reflection. A pinch of sympathy manages to infiltrate to my walled-off heart.

"Are you sure?" Kate asks.

"Positive." A tight smile curves his lips.

"Thank you. You're a lifesaver." Kate shifts the conversation to the wedding, but I'm still fixed on Rob's profile.

He finishes the wine in his glass and sets it aside. His gaze shifts to me, and I see exhaustion in the depths of his kind eyes.

I lean closer. "Rough day at the office?"

"You could say that." He drops his gaze to the half-empty plate on the table.

"Too many nurses to choose from?" I tease. It bothers me when he's in such a somber mood. I miss his smile and poke a little to stir the pot. "Did one of them shoot you down?"

"Damn it, Marcy." He shakes his head and pierces me with

a stern look. "Just sitting in your ivory tower judging everyone beneath you doesn't give you the right to make assumptions about my life. Or my job."

"I—"

"You're what? Sorry?" He scoffs. "Save it, all right? I'm not in the mood for your bullshit tonight."

My jaw drops when Rob shoves away from the table and stalks across the room. After he disappears through the archway into the bar, I turn to Kate and Arthur. Their stunned expressions mirror mine.

"What did you say to him?" Arthur narrows his eyes at me.

"Nothing. I…I made a joke…" My voice drifts off when my brother shakes his head.

"After all these years, you just can't ease up, can you?"

Shame settles in the pit of my gut. I drop my hands to my lap. "I didn't mean anything by it."

"You never do." Arthur stands and kisses Kate's forehead. "I'll be right back." He trails after his best friend without another word.

Damn it. I bite my lip and stifle the tears threatening to ruin my mascara.

Kate slides into Rob's seat and rests her hand on mine. "It's okay, hon. I'm sure he's just had a rough day at work. He didn't mean to take it out on you."

"Yeah, he did." I sniff. "I shouldn't have teased him like that. I thought it would make him laugh."

"Has he ever done that before?"

"Never."

"Hmm." Kate pats my hand. "How long have you known Rob?"

"Years." The memories flood my brain. I can still remember the first time I saw him. Young and determined. Handsome as hell. "He was premed at Georgetown, where he met my brother. Arthur brought him home for Christmas. I was seventeen."

I fell in love with him at seventeen, but he wouldn't give me the time of day.

Kate's eyes brighten. "You had a crush on him, didn't you?"

"Maybe a little one." I push aside my rising emotions. "But it vanished quickly. He wasn't interested in anything but studying medicine and chasing older women."

"What happened between you two?"

"Nothing." I straighten up and finish my wine. "He went on to med school, and I got married."

"When did you see Rob again?"

"The night I left my husband." The encounter is vivid in my mind. "Rob and Arthur helped me."

My body ached as I had dragged myself to my brother's doorstep. Arthur's horrified expression when he saw the extent of my injuries is forever seared in my brain. I begged him not to call the cops. But he insisted. I refused to go to the emergency room. So he called Rob.

The cops took my statement while Rob tended to the cuts on my arms and the bruises on my face. He never said a word. I could see how desperately he wanted to ask what happened, but he kept his mouth pressed in a thin line. Cold fury burned in his eyes. Both Rob and Arthur wanted to kill the bastard for what he had done to me. Their argument remains fixed in the darkest part of my psyche.

I push it aside and smile at Kate.

"It's okay, Marcy." Kate hugs me.

It's only then I realize I'm crying. I snatch the napkin and dab my eyes, cursing when the white linen comes away smeared with mascara. "Damn expensive shit should be waterproof."

Kate pulls away. Her tender gaze searches my face. "I'm sorry you had to go through such hell."

"Thanks, hon." I force a smile. "I'm stronger now because of it."

She knows the details of that night. Arthur told her. But even after ten years, I can't talk about it. I don't want to talk about it.

"You always give Rob a hard time." Kate treads carefully with her words. "Do you really hate him?"

Her question lingers, turning over again and again as I inspect it with curiosity. *Do I hate him?* No. But I don't want to examine the other emotions left behind. "No."

"Then why are you so mean to him?"

"Because he irritates me." I exhale sharply.

"Why?"

"I don't know." I twist the napkin in my hands. "He just gets under my skin. I don't like it."

Kate nods, understanding. "Maybe it's about time you two find some common ground. I don't know. Maybe you could be friends."

I scoff. "Rob and I aren't friends. Never will be."

"Why?"

"We have nothing in common."

"How do you know? Have you had a conversation with him that didn't end in one of you getting stitches?" She chuckles.

"No, and I'm not interested in being friends with Rob." It's true. Friendship is the last thing on my mind when it comes to Rob. I want more than that…

Nope, I'm locking that door right now. Not even entertaining those thoughts. I'm done with relationships.

"Then why are you upset that he snapped at you?"

Well, fuck. Isn't that the ultimate question? I toss the napkin on the table. "Because he's never done it before, and I'm worried he might go postal."

Kate's shrewd gaze fixes on me, and I pointedly ignore it.

"Are you going to be okay at the wedding tomorrow?" she asks.

"Yeah." I flag down the waiter and order another glass of wine. "Why wouldn't I be?"

"I know weddings aren't your thing." She beams. "But I'm thrilled to have you as my maid of honor."

"Well, don't expect any sappy speeches from me."

"I won't. I'm just glad you'll be there to celebrate with us."

I click my tongue. "You're lucky I love you and my brother enough to suffer through this."

Kate nudges my shoulder with hers. "I'm beyond lucky."

"Enough with the sentimental stuff—can we order dessert?"

"Yes, please." She bites her lip, hesitating. "Shouldn't we wait for Arthur and Rob?"

"They're on their own. I need some chocolate cake. Stat."

Kate laughs and waves to the waiter. She places the order for our dessert while I nurse my wine.

I should apologize to Rob. He's right; I don't know anything about his life or his job. For years, I've kept such a distance between us, it's hard not to be defensive.

What worries me most is this lingering concern for him. I don't want to think about Rob. I sure as hell don't want to worry about him. But I do.

Fuck. Years of erecting this perfectly structured wall around my heart, and now I'm trying to climb over it for a better view.

Rob and I aren't friends. I doubt we ever will be. If I ever open the door to that possibility, it will only be a matter of time before I find myself falling head over heels for him. Again.

I try to convince myself I never loved Rob. It was just a stupid, silly teenage crush. There was never anything between us, and there never will be.

I'm not interested in anything longer than a one-night stand, and Rob's not that kind of guy. He's a respectable doctor and a compassionate man. We have nothing in common and no future.

The waiter places a decadent piece of chocolate cake on the table in front of me. My mouth waters. It's a temptation, just like Rob. One taste will never be enough.

Ignoring the turmoil churning inside me, I indulge in the cake, knowing *it* won't come back to bite me in the ass.

Chapter Six
Rob

Regret hangs over me like a specter as I make my way through the restaurant.

I shouldn't have snapped at Marcy like that. But my restraint was already cracked, and having her beside me put unbearable tension on the weak points. There's no reason for me to take my shitty mood out on my friends. Shit, I'm an asshole.

After the day I've had, seeing her happy and healthy beside me should have infused me with gratitude. Instead, it unleashed a torrent of emotions I hadn't anticipated. Memories of Marcy covered in blood, sobbing in Arthur's arms, her struggle to find herself again after that asshole tore her apart. The rage resurfaced with a vengeance, and I wasn't prepared for the fallout.

Then she looks at me with those intoxicating eyes, and I'm lost. I want nothing more than to kiss her senseless and drag her back to my place. I want to make sure she's loved thoroughly for the rest of her fucking life. She deserves it.

But it doesn't matter. I could be the last man on the planet and Marcy would reject me.

Still doesn't give me the right to bite her head off for teasing. Fury curls like a ball in my chest, pressing on my sternum.

There's an empty spot at the bar. I take it and flag down the bartender. I've already had two glasses of wine. I know better than to compound my misery by dousing it with more alcohol.

"What can I get you?" the bartender asks.

"Tonic water."

He arches his brow in surprise but pours me the drink. My gaze is lost in the small bubbles floating to the top of the glass.

"What the hell was that?" Arthur's admonition echoes

behind me.

I turn to face him. He's an angry brick wall.

"It's been a shit day." I offer the lame excuse. Arthur doesn't buy it. We've known each other for too long. He can see right through me.

"Bullshit. I've seen you stressed to the breaking point. You've never taken it out on Marcy. Ever." Arthur keeps his voice low, but it's stern.

Words fail me. I stare into my glass.

"Whatever happened, she didn't deserve that."

"Don't you think I know that?" I growl, causing the man beside us to glance over suspiciously.

Damn it. I stand and move toward the shadowed hallway. Arthur follows. The moment we're alone, he crosses his arms.

"Then what the hell made you snap like that?"

I cradle the drink in one hand. My grip tightens as the earlier confrontation in the ER replays through my mind. "There was a patient today." A dull ache forms at the base of my skull. "A woman. We suspected domestic abuse. But…"

"But she didn't want help." Arthur finishes the thought for me.

I clench my jaw and nod. "The girl was terrified. She was the same age as Marcy when…"

"Rob." Arthur's posture softens, and he rests his hand on my shoulder. "You did the best you could."

"Did I?" My voice cracks. "She wouldn't even answer the questions herself. The bastard stood there, cocky and smug, while I took care of her injuries. The ones *he* caused."

"Do you have any proof he did it?"

"No." I hang my head and collapse against the wall. "And when I got her alone for the CAT scan, she still wouldn't talk."

"I can't imagine working in an environment where you're put in that position." Arthur leans against the wall beside me. "You offered. There's nothing more you could have done."

"I know. It's just…"

"Marcy."

"Yeah." I rub my hand over my face. The image is burned

into my brain. Every time a battered woman comes into my hospital, I see Marcy, broken and bleeding.

"The stress is too much, Rob. Maybe you should take a break. Step away from the intensity of working in the emergency room."

"I can't. It's my calling."

"Well, it's killing you. If you keep burning yourself out like this, you're gonna have a heart attack before you reach fifty."

I scoff, but he's right; the burden is overwhelming. "It's all I have, Arthur. It's my life."

"I didn't say give up medicine, but maybe you should consider alternate employment possibilities." He pauses as though pondering those options. "You could easily start your own practice. Keep office hours. Take a vacation once in a while."

Alone? No thanks. While his suggestion makes sense, it would leave me miserable. If I take away my work, the only thing I have is the gnawing ache for a woman who doesn't want me. I'm fucking pathetic.

"Are you going to be okay for the wedding tomorrow morning?" Arthur's question breaks through my mental fog.

"Yeah. I'll be there."

"You'd better not make my sister cry at my fucking wedding. I don't care how long we've been friends. I'll kill you with my bare hands."

My body tenses at the undercurrent of his tone. He means it. "I promise I'll be in a better mindset. I just need some rest."

"Good." He straightens and offers his hand. I take it. "Now, let's go back and get some dessert."

"Fine." I follow him back to the table. My mood hasn't changed, but I force a smile when we return to find the ladies enjoying chocolate cake without us.

Arthur resumes his seat, and Kate abandons the spot I had occupied before my outburst.

"Everything okay?" Kate asks, sitting beside Arthur.

"We're good," Arthur responds, glancing at me.

Marcy takes a bite of cake, her gaze fixed on the half-eaten slice before her. Her shoulders are tense.

Apologize, you idiot, my mind screams. But nothing comes out. Fuck. My mood takes another nose dive.

I manage to squeak out an apology and excuse myself from the table. My mumbled apology and excuse seem to mollify Kate. But Arthur continues to eat his cake in silence, watching me.

"Goodnight, Marcy."

She waves her hand, unable to meet my gaze. Shit.

I fucked this up. Damn it. How do I rebuild the tenuous bridge between us?

The duration of my commute home, I ponder all the ways in which I can fix the fragile relationship between Marcy and me. It may be too late. She's already made it perfectly clear how she feels about me. Maybe it's time I take a hint and give her the space she asks for.

When I reach my apartment, I strip on the way to the bathroom. I've already showered once, but I need it again. I feel dirty. But a shower won't cure this. Nothing will.

Leaning against the cool tile, I let the warm water slide over me. I imagine it's the featherlight touch of Marcy's lips and fingertips. The fantasy takes root and I'm transported.

My cock hardens at the mental image of Marcy naked and wet as she explores me. I refrain from seeking release, no matter how much I need it.

No. I shake my head and turn off the shower. I can't keep doing this. Dreaming of Marcy and all the delicious things I want to do with her—it's torment. It has been for years.

I've dated other women. I've tried to find someone who fits my world, who understands me. But they're not Marcy.

Her comment about the nurses cut deeper than she realized. I've had nurses throw themselves at me. Hell, I've had other doctors flirt with me while on duty. But I'm a professional. I take my job seriously.

I don't mix work and pleasure.

The fact that she would even think I'm that kind of man hurts like hell. She knows me better than that, even if she won't admit it.

It took every ounce of strength I possess not to tell her the truth. She's the only woman I want, the reason I breathe. I would do anything for her if she would only ask. Instead, I let my overwhelmed emotions get the better of me, and I hurt the woman I love.

I'm no better than that asshole who abused her.

Burdened by this knowledge, I climb into bed and pull the sheet up. The darkness surrounds me, and I succumb to it. Marcy's waiting for me in my dreams, but they quickly turn to nightmares when she abandons me completely.

CHAPTER SEVEN
MARCY

"How do I look?" Kate spins around, her ankle-length skirt lifting like a flag on a summer breeze. The gown is a bold choice—A-line with a sweetheart neck, without the popular puffed organza sleeves and over-sequined fabric. When she asked me to help her design it, I thought she was crazy. Turns out I was the crazy one. It's lovely and classic and suits her to perfection, accentuating her generous curves.

"You look gorgeous." A lump forms in my throat as I adjust the pearls nestled against her throat. "Arthur's going to flip when he sees you."

"Well, this is your handiwork." Her face turns pink. "Thank you for everything."

"Of course. We're sisters now." I kiss her cheek, then busy myself with packing the makeup kit to keep from making a sentimental fool of myself.

Sunlight streams in the windows of the Empire State Building, illuminating Kate like an angel sent from heaven. My heart twists at the sight of her in her wedding gown with a crown of flowers in her curled hair. She looks lovely.

I'm happy for them. Truly.

Even though the circumstances of Kate's appearance in our lives seem a little farfetched, I can't help but be grateful for the twist of fate. This should be a joyous day. My brother is getting married to the love of his life. And I'm left with this gaping hole in my chest, the burden of painful memories haunting me from the past.

Marriage should be a partnership. A uniting of two souls who were made for each other. At least, that's the fairy tale. But marriage left me shattered and floundering. The institution lost all its meaning after my hellish experience.

Gladys, Arthur's secretary, appears in the doorway. "They're ready for you on the observation deck."

"Thanks, Gladys." Kate turns to face me, her eyes sparkling and her wide smile infectious. "Shall we go?"

I step to the side and sweep a dramatic bow. "After you."

Kate grabs the bouquet of lilies and roses sitting on Arthur's desk and swans out of the office. I follow, making sure the doors are locked behind me. When we reach the elevators, Kate takes my hand.

"Nervous?" I press the button for the observation deck.

"Yeah." Her hand trembles, and I squeeze it tight.

"Those nerves will disappear the moment you see Arthur. I promise." My comforting words ease her trembling.

They decided to have the ceremony in the same place where it all began on New Year's Day—the Empire State Building. Some would say it's romantic, like an homage to that old film, *An Affair to Remember*. I'm just thrilled they're opting for a non-traditional wedding. I'm pretty sure I'd burst into flames if I set foot in a church.

When the elevator dings, I release her hand. The doors open, and Arthur's business partner, Victor, stands waiting for us. He offers his arm to Kate.

"May I?"

Tears well up in her eyes. "I would be honored, Victor. Thank you."

Kate slides her arm through his, and they step out into the bright May sunlight.

I slip around them and make my way toward the small area they transformed into a lovely, romantic oasis. A dozen chairs lay on either side of the makeshift red-carpet aisle. At the end of the aisle, near the railing, stands my brother in a dapper black tuxedo. Beside him stands the pastor, and off to the side is Rob, wearing a matching tuxedo and a bright blue bow tie.

My heart flutters at the sight of him standing there. Damn it, why is he so handsome?

Soft strains of music fill the air. The string quartet is an elegant touch. I make my way up the aisle and take my position to the left of the priest.

When I turn to watch Kate's procession, I'm struck speechless. Her radiant smile only compounds the effervescent joy pouring off her in waves. She grips Victor's arm tightly as she walks down the aisle to Arthur, her eyes shining bright. When they reach the small dais, she hugs Victor and kisses his cheek. Tears roll down her face.

Arthur takes her hand as she steps forward to take her place beside him. She turns and hands me the bouquet.

I step closer, take the flowers, and place a handkerchief in her hand.

My gaze skims over the crowd as Kate turns to Arthur. There's only a handful of guests. Victor and his extremely pregnant wife, who looks like she's about to burst. Gladys, Cyril, and a few other friends of the family. The music fades before coming to an end.

"Dearly beloved…" The pastor begins the ceremony, and I clutch the flowers tightly in my hands.

These words. They're painful. They dredge up memories I would rather leave buried at the bottom of the Hudson River. I close my eyes, wishing I had something to focus on. Something to distract me from the twisting, gnawing ache that rips my head and heart apart.

When I open my eyes, my gaze fixes like a laser on Rob. I inhale sharply.

He's not watching the ceremony or the guests. His attention is focused on me.

Only me.

The pastor recites the vows, but it's background noise. Every fiber of my being is on fire. Rob never wavers. It's like *we* are standing on the dais before the pastor and the congregation. I brace myself for panic to overwhelm me, but it never comes. Instead, a peace settles around me. We're transported, the two of us, to a stolen moment in time amid family and friends.

Kate and Arthur repeat the vows. As they speak the words and exchange the rings, Rob flexes his jaw, pressing his lips together in a thin line. It's almost as though he wants to speak but stops himself. Strange.

"I now pronounce you husband and wife," the pastor announces. "You may kiss the bride."

Arthur sweeps Kate into a passionate embrace. The crowd erupts in cheers and applause. Rob and I remain steadfast, our gazes locked.

Kate spins around and hugs me tight, breaking the spell. "Now we're truly sisters!"

She takes her bouquet and links her arm through Arthur's. They make their way back down the aisle, greeting their guests and smiling while the quartet plays an uplifting tune.

Rob closes the gap between us and offers his arm. "May I escort you to the reception?"

My throat closes. "I…need to take care of something first." Brushing past him, I head for the elevator.

My heart pounds as I press the button for the ground floor. I lied. The only thing I need is to put some distance between Rob and me.

My hand rests against my chest; I will my heart to stop racing. What the hell just happened? One minute I'm at my brother's wedding, and the next, I'm tangled in some staring contest with Rob.

No. It was more than that. The intensity of his gaze remains firmly fixed in my mind. There was no mask. No hiding the hunger I saw in the depths of his eyes. He didn't flinch. Didn't blink. That single-minded determination, open and bare for all the world to see. Has it always been there?

The car reaches the ground floor, and I hail a cab. During the ride to the restaurant, my mind spins.

After the way he reacted at dinner last night, I thought Rob had finally had enough of my sarcasm and biting wit. I didn't expect a resolution—or even an apology. But when he abandoned us so quickly, I had the distinct impression he wanted to be as far from me as possible.

The way he looked at me during the ceremony, though, told me there is something else going on. I swallow and lean my head back against the seat. Do I even want to know what it is?

Uncertainty curls inside me, and I wonder if I could possibly get away with skipping the reception altogether.

No. Arthur and Kate would be disappointed. Besides, they're leaving right after the reception. Their bags are packed and their flight leaves tonight.

The car pulls up to the restaurant. I manage to keep my composure as I go into the building and find the small ballroom reserved for their reception. The decorations are minimalistic but lovely. I admire the pink-tipped orange roses and white calla lilies nestled in dark green ferns in the crystal vases on each table. A banner hangs across the bride and groom's table. *Congratulations, Mr. and Mrs. Maxwell.*

My heart takes another hit. I might have to see a doctor after this. *Rob?* No. I pinch my eyes closed. I most certainly do not need to see *that* doctor.

I make my way to the ladies' powder room, where I collapse on a velvet-cushioned lounge chair. What the hell am I doing here? This is supposed to be their special day, and I'm having a full-on heart attack.

The time alone gives me a chance to collect my thoughts.

I can do this. It's only for a few hours, then I can go home and get back to business as usual. No problem. I just have to avoid Rob until then. Easy.

Gladys, Victor and his wife, and a few other guests have arrived by the time I return to the ballroom. Kate and Arthur enter, and I'm struck by how perfect they are for each other.

I find a seat at a table near a huge potted plant, far from the commotion. With such an intimate affair, it's difficult to blend into the crowd. Kate waves when she spots me. I wave back.

Where's the bar? I scan the room and frown when Rob appears at the entrance. As if drawn by a freakishly large magnet, his gaze homes in, directly on me. Fuck.

I shift uncomfortably, wishing I could dissolve into the carpet.

The familiar strains of REO Speedwagon filter over the speakers. Shit. It's my favorite song. Kate and Arthur are on the dance floor, swaying in time to the ballad.

Rob crosses the floor, his gaze riveted on me like I'm the only person in the room. He offers his hand. "Dance with me? Please."

"Fine." The word slips from my traitorous mouth.

Then it's too late. Rob takes my hand and leads me toward the dance floor.

My body thrums with need at his touch. When he rests his palm on my waist, I bite my lip. His warm hand engulfs mine as our movements fall in time with the music. I've never danced with Rob before. I imagined it once, long ago, when I was a naive teenager.

But I'm not a teenager or naive anymore.

He pulls me closer, and I stifle a moan before it betrays me.

"Marcy." His warm breath brushes my cheek.

I try to focus on anything but him, knowing if I meet his eyes, I won't be able to hide the desire burning inside me. "What?"

"I owe you an apology for my behavior last night."

I become viscerally aware of his proximity when my pulse spikes and my chest constricts.

He sighs. "I had a stressful day and I shouldn't have taken it out on you. I'm sorry."

Rob apologized. Hell must have frozen over.

What on Earth do I say to that?

CHAPTER EIGHT
ROB

"I understand." Her grip tightens on my shoulder, and I'm desperate to hold on with both hands to draw her flush against me. "Your job is stressful. I shouldn't have made such a stupid joke."

"Sarcastic comments are your trademark, Marcy." I soak up her warmth. "I'd be worried if you hadn't responded that way."

A small smile settles on her lips. "Still, I'm sorry."

"Already forgiven." My hand slides to the base of her spine, and I pull her closer.

Marcy softens and rests her head against my shoulder.

I'm trying my damnedest to keep the inferno under control, but having her in my arms is pushing me to the limit. I've dreamed of this moment for as long as I've known her—holding her close, keeping her safe. Marcy might be an independent woman, but she's not a machine. She's flesh and blood…and all heart when she deems someone worthy.

I want to be worthy. More than anything.

The song ends and another ballad begins. We continue dancing, spinning around on the dance floor. If she takes a half step closer, she'll know exactly how much I want her. My cock is rock hard. I'm glad I kept my jacket on. If I remove it now, the whole assembly will see the effect she has on me.

Part of me wants to tease her, to bait her into the sharp banter she embraces so easily. But I don't want to break this tender moment.

No. I finally have Marcy where I want her. Peaceful in my arms.

There's a soft tap on my shoulder. "Excuse me, Dr. Thompson?"

The magic moment is shattered. Marcy comes to a stop, and we both turn to the intruding party. It's one of the restaurant staff, looking quite repentant for interrupting our dance.

"Yes, that's me."

"There's a call for you, sir."

Marcy drops her hold on me, and the loss of her touch strikes me with the force of a lightning bolt. "Go ahead. I'll be here when you get back."

Those words lodge in my brain, and it short-circuits. Have we finally taken a step forward? I nod at Marcy and follow the man off the dance floor to the front of the restaurant. He gestures to the phone behind the partition.

"Dr. Thompson speaking."

"It's Summer." Her harried voice carries through the phoneline. Something's wrong.

"What's going on?"

"Sorry to interrupt, but I need you here. Stat." She takes a deep breath. "Grace is back."

"What happened?" My body tenses, and adrenaline dumps into my system.

"I don't know, but it's bad. How fast can you get here?"

"Ten minutes." I glance around the room, searching for someone from our party. Shit. I don't have time to waste. I'll apologize later. They'll understand. "I'll need clean scrubs."

"I'll have them waiting in the locker room. Hurry."

I hang up the phone and dart from the restaurant. Fortunately, I'm able to snag a cab and get to the hospital in five minutes. I murmur a prayer of thanks that Arthur and Kate chose a restaurant in our neighborhood.

By the time I walk into the ER, Summer's waiting at the entrance. She fills me in as we walk to the locker rooms.

"She came in an hour ago by ambulance. Unconscious." Summer keeps her voice low as I strip out of my suit. She hangs it up while I pull on scrubs. "I think there may be internal bleeding." She lists what they've already done and the meds they've administered.

I pull the top on and follow her out of the room. "Where's

her husband?"

"Down at the police station." Summer stops speaking, but I can tell there's more to the story. She doesn't want to tell me everything.

I can't blame her. Fury is pulsing through me, red hot. I'm about to rip this building apart.

"Summer. Tell me."

She groans but finally relents. "Cops showed up for a suspected domestic altercation. Found Grace unconscious and called the ambulance."

"Is he under arrest?" My hands flex into fists. He's lucky he's not here because I'd fucking kill him myself.

"No, but they're investigating what happened."

"As they should. It's better he's not here." I head down the hall. "Where is she?"

"Exam room four."

I stop outside the door. Keeping my voice low and my emotions contained, I ask, "Is there anyone here to advocate for her?"

"No. She's alone."

"Fuck." I take a deep breath to calm myself. I need a level head before I go in. "Okay."

I'm her advocate. The unspoken words take up space in my brain, expanding until they consume me with determination. I push aside the curtain and step into the room.

My heart plummets.

Grace lays quietly on the gurney. The wires and tubes attached to her look like something out of a science fiction film. I should be used to it, but no one should be complacent about seeing a young woman in such a way. An individual who should be full of life and vitality has been transformed into a bruised and battered victim of her circumstances.

Like Marcy had been.

Shit. I shove the thoughts aside and allow myself to fall into a familiar rhythm. I'm a doctor damn it. I can help her. I can save her.

I flip through a mental checklist as I examine her. Oxygen,

fluids, medication, all good. Heartrate, elevated and irregular. The bruises on her face are now two distinct shades. Yellow—from the aging ones—and deep purple and red. Those are fresh. Fuck.

My examination leads me down a dark path. The suspected injury from yesterday seems to have worsened. There's hemorrhaging beneath the skin of her abdomen and chest.

Summer watches from the other side of the bed with a worried expression. "What do you want to do?"

"I want a full CAT scan. The swelling on her face looks like it may be a fracture. I also want bloodwork done. What's her type?"

"A-positive."

"Okay, let's make sure we have some on hand."

"Got it." Summer darts from the room. I can hear her barking orders on the other side of the curtain.

I rest my hand on Grace's. "Don't worry. We'll take care of you. You're safe now."

A crew appears and wheels her down the hall to get the tests I requested. I follow behind, going through all the possibilities in my mind. I was on call today, but they didn't actually need me. There's no logical reason for me to be here.

Except that Grace needs me. She needs someone who cares. Someone to fight for her, damn it.

As they do the CAT scan, I watch the monitors. Shit. Liver and spleen look like they're damaged. There's a lot of subdermal hemorrhaging, and it's filling her abdominal cavity. I grab the phone.

"Yeah, Dr. Thompson here. Page the trauma surgeon and have an OR prepped for surgery, stat."

"Yes, sir." The nurse on the other end of the line doesn't question me when I give her the details.

I hang up the phone.

The tech sitting behind the console glances at me. "Should I finish the scan?"

"Yes. Finish it."

I analyze the results before stepping into action. Mandibular fracture. Hairline fracture of the cervical spine. Subdermal hemorrhaging. Fuck. Did he hit her with a baseball bat?

Grace is in critical condition. It's a blessing she's unconscious. The pain would be excruciating. I help the trio of nurses wheel her back to the ER while we wait for the surgical team to prepare. We have to get the bleeding under control before we can address the other issues.

Summer joins me when we return to the ER. "What do we have?"

I fill her in. My composure slips when I see Grace on the table. So fragile. So alone. I've worked in the ER for years, seen similar cases a million times, but nothing prepares me for the slap in the face I feel when I see the damage this poor, sweet girl has endured. I could have stopped it.

No. I can't think that way. I need to focus. With a deep breath, I clear my head. Summer comes beside me, a silent but steadfast support.

I'm mentally drained, but I can't give up on Grace. I won't. She deserves better.

Grace's vitals drop. Her oxygen plummets and she seizes. Her battered body relinquishes the fight.

"Code blue!" I shout before Summer and I spring into action, screaming orders, directing the chaos that descends on the claustrophobic room.

When her heart stops, I choke back a sob. No, damn it. Don't die on me.

Summer grabs the crash cart and we attempt to resuscitate her, but nothing helps.

The horrific flatline tone echoes through the room.

She's gone.

Exhausted, we step away from the table as a nurse calls the time of death. A horrifying numbness settles around me.

I cradle her cheek in my hand. "I'm sorry, Grace."

Summer nudges me with her elbow. I take a deep breath and leave her.

She's at peace now. He can't hurt her anymore. She's safe.

"Hey, you did the best you could." Summer claps me on the

shoulder after we clean up.

"Yeah." She's right. I did. But knowing that doesn't stop me from dropping into my own pit of self-deprecation. I could have done more. I could have stopped him the first time she came into my ER, broken and scared. I toss my scrubs into the bin and head for the shower.

No matter how hard I scrub, I can't wash away the shame of my failure. Tears mingle with the water running over my face.

What if it had been Marcy on that gurney?

I can't dwell on that. Grace isn't Marcy. Marcy escaped that fate. But it doesn't stop me from wondering what would have happened had Arthur and I not been there to help her cut ties with her ex.

Somehow, I manage to scrape myself together. Summer tells me she'll put the file on my desk for Monday morning. Everything blurs together as I make my way home.

What started as a joyful day, full of hope and new beginnings, evolved into an epic disaster. I feel like I'm on a flaming rollercoaster and it's just gone off the rails, hurtling toward certain doom. Maybe a good night's sleep will help…but I doubt it.

It's nearly ten when I get home. I change and grab a beer from the fridge before collapsing on the couch in the darkness.

Kate and Arthur are on their way to Italy. Marcy…fuck. She probably thinks I'm an asshole for ditching her at the reception. I would give anything to start the day over and not blow it.

The image of Marcy in her hot pink, sequined gown, standing beside Kate on the top of the Empire State Building is burned into my mind. I couldn't stop staring at her. I wanted her more in that moment than I've wanted anything in my whole life.

I wanted her to speak those vows to me.

But I'll settle for another dance. Another chance to prove I'm serious about her.

I only hope I haven't fucked it up beyond repair.

CHAPTER NINE
MARCY

Rob never came back.

The wedding was two days ago, and Arthur and Kate are safe in Rome, enjoying their honeymoon, while I'm lying in bed on a Monday morning replaying Rob's apology in my mind. I wrench myself out of bed and head for the shower.

Something changed between Rob and me on that dance floor. His apology. The way he held me as we moved to the music. It's like the Earth shifted, the sun now rising in the west and setting in the east. My whole world feels off-center, but not in a bad way.

I waited for him to come back to the reception, even ordered him a drink. But after two hours, I drank it and plastered a fake smile on my lips. I was there to celebrate Arthur and Kate's wedding, not to moon over Rob. I thought I had put that childish crush far behind me, but whatever spark ignited between us on the roof of the Empire State Building followed us to the reception.

Warmth floods me at the memory. I can't imagine what would have happened had we not been interrupted. Would I have confessed my longstanding infatuation with him? Given into the heat building with every sway to the music?

He promised he'd come back, but he never did. I can't help but wonder if it's my fault.

I shouldn't be thinking about him. Whatever feelings I have for him—whether they're lust or something more—should sit firmly on the shelf. I don't want to complicate our tenuous friendship…if I can even call it that.

The spray of hot water washes the need away, but the thoughts remain in the back of my mind. I need to work. It will keep me distracted…I mean focused on what's important.

Last night, I got a call from Donna. Studio 35 has requested us to take care of their guests this week since their previously booked stylist had a family emergency. It's a last-minute addition, and I'll have to split my stylists between two locations. But I can't say no to Studio 35. They host celebrity news interviews as well as MTV. I'd be insane to turn them down. I've worked with them in the past, and they're top-notch. We'll just have to make a few adjustments to fit it all in.

Somehow, I manage to get myself looking halfway decent, and I head to the station. The commute is minimal since both locations are close to my apartment. I make it in the door at five to eight.

"Hold the elevator!"

A massive hand grabs the doors before they snap closed. I breathe a sigh of relief when they open.

"Thanks." I nearly trip when I reach the elevator.

Vic Simmons is holding the door. A smile curves his mouth when I step into the carriage. "Fancy meeting you here."

"Likewise."

The door closes, and I realize we're the only two people in the elevator. I fix my gaze on the mirrored surface before me.

"What floor?" he asks.

"Twelve."

He drops his hand, and I see the button is already illuminated. My gaze shifts to his. "You're going to twelve too?"

"Yup. I have an interview for an upcoming action film." He shoves his hands into his pockets.

The man's shoulders are so broad, I feel like he takes up half the elevator. But it could just be his presence.

"Oh, congrats on the new film." I straighten the bag strap on my shoulder.

"Thank you." He glances at me in reflection. "You look lovely today."

My face heats, and I nearly choke on my gum. What are words? I can't seem to string two of them together. He complimented me…I'm wearing a white leather skirt and a hot pink top. I grabbed them in a rush, and I look like a fucking mess with big hair and sparkly eye shadow. Granted, I'm supposed to look that way. It's all the rage right now, but it doesn't scream sex appeal to me.

Judging by the way Vic is drinking me in, I'd say it *does* scream that to him. And I'm not completely wigged out by it either.

"You're quite good at your job." Vic flashes a disarming smile. "Do you enjoy it?"

"Totally." I snap my gum and try to play it cool. I'm a thirty-five-year-old woman spazzing out over a hot actor giving me a compliment. What the hell is wrong with me? "I mean, I've always been into fashion. Why not make it a career, right?"

"Absolutely. You should do what you love what makes you happy."

"Well, it didn't start that way. It was more about paying the bills." I glance at the numbers above the door to distract me from his charming presence.

"I can understand that." He chuckles, and the sound ripples through me. "I wasn't always the successful leading man you see before you."

"Get out of town. I never would have guessed."

"It's true." He sighs dramatically. "But I've been fortunate to turn my passion into my livelihood. Something we have in common."

The elevator reaches the twelfth floor, and the doors slide open. A vague connection doesn't mean anything, does it?

"I guess I'll see you later." I step from the carriage.

"I look forward to it." Vic gives a jaunty little salute and heads down the hall.

A cluster of people surround him, and I'm left staring after him in confusion.

Was Vic flirting with me? Or am I just a hotbed of lust-fueled coals left simmering after my dance with Rob? I shake off the lingering tension and weave my way through the studio to the dressing rooms.

Liana glances up when I walk in the door. "Finally! I'm

freaking out here." She bustles around me with five hangers dangling from her fingertips. "I wasn't sure which ones we would—"

"Honey." I take the clothes and put them on the rack. "Take a breath. We got this. Okay?"

"I know. I just hate when we spread ourselves this thin." She bites her lip. "Do you know who we're styling today?"

"I haven't seen the list yet, but Vic Simmons is here." I waggle my brows.

Liana's eyes widen, and I swear there are hearts dancing in her pupils. "He's a dreamboat."

"He is easy on the eyes, I won't deny that." I skim through the selections and make mental notes on what we have on hand. "Plus he's charming. I ran into him in the elevator."

"You were alone with him?" Liana grabs my arm. "Tell me everything."

"Not much to tell, honestly." I warm from the inside out. "Although, I think he was flirting with me."

"Whoa." Liana gapes, her crimped hair falling across her eyes. "Did he ask you out?"

"No." I wave my hand and laugh. "Like I would ever date a client. You know me better than that."

"Yeah, I know all about your rules, but this is *Vic Simmons* we're talking about here."

"You act like that's supposed to mean something to me, Liana?"

A knock at the door interrupts us. It's the stage manager with the list of clients. I take it and tell him to send the first client in when they arrive.

Liana snatches the list from my hand. "So back to Vic. You gonna give him a shot or what?"

"For the hundredth time, I don't date clients. Period."

"Maybe you should break your rule this one time?" Liana winks. "Come on…just one little date."

"He hasn't even asked me out. Don't you think you're getting ahead of yourself here?"

"He'll ask." Liana nods in certainty. "I saw the way he

looked at you last week."

"Oh stop, Liana. Seriously, I'm too old for these games." I rifle through the garment rack and pull a few dresses for the first client.

Another knock at the door saves me from Liana's incessant nagging. "Come in," I call without turning.

Liana nudges me in the ribs.

"What?" I spin around to find Vic standing in the doorway. "Oh, it's you." I replace the gowns and pull a casual menswear ensemble from the rack, taking into account his dark hair and bright blue eyes as I select the colors.

"I'm gonna go grab that box I left in the hallway," Liana mutters as she slips out the door, clearly breaking the rule she knows I live by.

For the second time today, I'm left alone with Vic Simmons. Typically, I'd be worried about being alone with my client, but after the ride in the elevator, I'm oddly at ease with his presence. That should be a flaming red flag all by itself.

"Here. These should fit. I'll just wait outside for you to change."

"I hope I don't make you uncomfortable…" He seems to search for my name like I never gave it to him, but he knows exactly what it is.

I humor him regardless. "Marcy." I clear my throat. "And no, you don't. I just wanted to give you some privacy."

"How thoughtful."

My heart flips at his sheepish smile. The hell is wrong with me?

I step outside and lean against the door. There's no sign of Liana in the hallway. Traitor. She bailed on purpose, trying to play matchmaker. I should fire her ass. But I won't. She's practically family.

After a few minutes, I knock on the door. Vic opens it.

I gasp at the sight of him in a blue polo with a flipped collar. The tailored tan slacks perfectly hug his thighs.

"You're sure about this?" He gestures to the shirt.

"For sure." I smooth the collar, and my fingertips brush his neck. With a gasp, I drop my hands. "You look gnarly."

"Is that a good thing?" he asks with a laugh.

"Totally." My gaze skims the length of him, one last appraisal of my styling before I send him out on camera.

"Marcy." His voice cuts through the silence.

"Yeah?" I snap my gum and meet his gaze.

"Would you have dinner with me next week?"

"I don't know, Vic." My heart does two somersaults, then lands like a rock in my stomach. "I don't date clients." Even as I say it, my traitorous heart pushes back against my conscience, demanding I pursue whatever this is.

He pulls a card from his wallet and hands it to me. "My number, in case you change your mind."

"Thanks." I take the card and slip it into my bra. His gaze follows the movement. "But I told you, I don't date clients."

"Well, it doesn't have to be a date. Just two people having dinner, getting to know each other."

That grin devastates me with its undeniable charm. Warning bells should be going off in my head, but I'm too smitten to care.

I tap my chin. "I'll think about it."

The stage manager pops his head in the door. "Vic, you're on in five."

"Got it. Thanks." He shoves his hands in his pockets after the manager leaves. "I'm in town for two more weeks. Just call if you change your mind."

Something's wrong with me because I can't find a single response in my brain. It's not until Vic leaves the room that I can breathe again. What the hell just happened?

I can't seriously be considering going out with Vic? That would break every promise I've made to myself. No relationships. No dating. Nothing serious.

Definitely no dating clients.

Am I honestly giving this serious thought?

What about Rob? What about what happened Saturday on the dance floor?

No. I'm not letting Rob influence any decisions I make pertaining to my sex life. He doesn't get a say.

When Liana returns, I play it off. She doesn't need to know about Vic's invitation. No one does because it's none of their damn business.

Shit. Why does this have to be so damn difficult?

CHAPTER TEN
ROB

I miss my bed. Don't get me wrong, Arthur's penthouse has a better view of the city and more space, but it's not the same as my shoebox apartment and lumpy mattress.

Being here reminds me of Marcy. I haven't seen or spoken to her since the wedding reception. Since our dance. Between my regular shifts and overtime, I can't seem to get a break this week. This is the first free moment I've had, and I'm taking it to relax and read a book.

I set aside the Chinese takeout menu and sink back into the couch cushions. Dinner's on the way, and I've disconnected the phone. Tabby jumps onto the empty space beside me. Her inquisitive green eyes search my face.

"Hello, sweetheart." I scratch her head, and she arches into my touch, rubbing her face against my hand. Her purring resonates through my fingertips. She mews in response and climbs onto my lap.

"Can't let you languish here alone, can we?" I stroke her fur, and she curls against my chest. "Affectionate thing, aren't you?"

Her sweet little mew melts my heart. I'm not typically an animal person, but Tabby's been wonderful company these past few days. It's nice knowing someone's waiting for me to come home, craving my attention.

Am I talking about a cat or something else?

Even though Marcy keeps me at arm's length and seizes every opportunity to sink her claws into me, I know it's because she's scared she'll lose that precarious balance she's fought so hard to gain. Her protective instincts run deep.

I turn on the television while we wait for the food. Tabby purrs contentedly against me while I flip through the channels searching for something worth watching. I pause on the local news. I don't really care what it is; I really just want some background noise.

A knock at the door pulls me from my search.

"That was fast," I murmur to Tabby and set her aside. They knock again just as I reach the landing. "I'm coming."

When I open the door, my heart flips twice. "Marcy." I lean against the doorway and drink her in.

"Rob." The neon top and sparkly gray pants don't detract from her natural glow. She looks like a rock star and every fantasy I've ever had. Even her eyes shimmer in the hall light. "Can I come in?"

"Yeah, sure." I open the door and step aside. "You just get off work?"

"Yup." She brushes past me, and the scent of her perfume and Aqua Net lingers in her wake. A bag dangles from her hand. "I forgot to drop off my wedding gift. Figured I would do it now while I have a chance."

"Busy week?" I ask, closing the door before Tabby can escape into the hall.

"Totally." Marcy snaps her gum and ventures into the living room. "I'm gonna put this on the counter so they'll see it when they get back."

"Be my guest." Tabby weaves through my legs. I scoop her into my arms and scratch behind her ears. I might be grasping at straws, but Marcy showing up like this seems like a sign. I should take a chance, right?

"You got plans for dinner?"

"No, why?" Marcy sets the bag on the counter and turns. "Are you cooking?"

"Not tonight. I just put in an order for takeout." Tabby's purring amplifies my heartbeat in my ears. "I ordered double if you're hungry."

A slow grin curves on the sinful lips I've imagined wrapped around my cock. "Are you asking me to stay for dinner?"

"I am. But if you'd rather not spend time in my presence, I understand."

Marcy crosses the gap between us to pet Tabby, who's contentedly cradled in my arms, purring up a storm. "I'll stay, but only if you tell me why you didn't come back to the reception on Saturday."

Pain flashes through me at the reminder, but she deserves an explanation for my disappearance. "Deal."

Grinning, she takes Tabby from my arms and nuzzles her face in the cat's fur. I've never been jealous of an animal in my life, but here I am, glaring at Tabby. Marcy settles on the couch with the affectionate kitten.

I'm about to speak when a knock at the door cuts me off. This time it's the delivery boy. I take the food, give him a little more than the cost of the meal, and bid him farewell. Burdened with two bags of takeout, I return to the living room and set them on the coffee table.

Marcy puts Tabby on the couch and scoots closer. "What'd you order? The usual?"

I arch my brow at her. "How would you know what I like?"

"Rob, seriously." She scoffs and pulls out the container of lo mein. "You've been friends with my brother since I was in high school. I know a lot more about you than you think I do."

"I doubt that." I snort and sit down beside her.

She hands me the broccoli and beef. I snatch chopsticks off the table with a huff.

"Try me." She opens her chopsticks and takes a bite of the noodles.

"Fine." I push aside the broccoli, searching for the beef. "What's my mom's first name?"

"Martha." She slurps down another bite. "Come on, give me a hard one."

"Okay. My favorite sport?"

"Baseball." She shakes her head. "You played in high school and college. Your favorite team is the Yankees."

I narrow my gaze. Confidence oozes out of her. She's practically gloating. "All right. I didn't always want to be a doctor. What did I want to be before I went to college?" There's no way she can possibly know this. I've never told another soul.

Not even Arthur.

Marcy stops chewing and levels her gaze with mine. She holds it while she thinks. I can see the flecks of gold in her eyes. It's taking all my restraint to not hook my hand around her neck, pull her close, and kiss the smirk right off her lips.

"A spy."

Astonishment floods me. How the fuck...

I jab the chopsticks in her direction. "How the hell did you know that?"

"I can read your mind." She gasps dramatically before chuckling and taking another bite of her noodles.

"No, seriously. I never told anyone that."

"Like I said before, I know you better than you think I do." She winks, and my passive desire increases to a simmering boil.

I stuff a piece of broccoli in my mouth. If I hadn't been head over heels for this woman already, I certainly would be smitten now. We lapse into silence as we eat. I grab two beers from the fridge and pop the tops.

She takes one and sighs in contentment. "Thanks for dinner. It hit the spot."

"Thanks for keeping me company." I salute her before taking a drink.

"So what happened Saturday night? Why'd you bail?"

"Hospital called." I hesitate, wondering how much I should actually tell her. There were too many similarities between Grace and Marcy. I swallow the lump in my throat. "There was an emergency with one of my patients."

"Oh no." Her teasing demeanor fades at my revelation. "I should've known it was important. You'd never bail on my brother like that if it weren't." She spins the bottle in her hands. "Was everything okay?"

I shake my head, unable to find the words, and hide my face behind the beer bottle. "She died."

"Oh, Rob. I'm so sorry." Marcy's hand rests on my knee. "I'm sure you did everything you could."

If I had a nickel for every time I heard that phrase, I'd be richer than Arthur. I sniff and tip my head back. "Yeah, well...it wasn't enough."

Marcy bites her lip and takes my hand. The touch infuses me with comfort and hope. I squeeze it and smile.

"Thanks for trying to cheer me up, Marcy." I sigh. "It's part of the job. It fucking sucks, but I'll get over it. I can't save them all."

Marcy rests her head on my shoulder and threads her fingers in mine. "You'll try though. If I know you, you'll do your damnedest to save every last person who comes to you for help."

"You know it." I chuckle at how well she does know me.

"It's gotta be better than being an international spy." Her words are soft, but I hear them clearly enough.

"I don't know. Travel the world, dine in fancy restaurants, stay in the world's classiest hotels, make love to the most beautiful women in the universe. It's a toss-up."

She shoves her weight against me. "You watch too many Bond films."

That's when it clicks. "Ahh, now it makes sense."

"What?" She draws back and looks at me, confused.

"How you knew I wanted to be a spy."

"What?" Her cheeks turn pink. "I've seen your collection of Ian Fleming novels, and I know you've seen every James Bond film."

"You're observant, I'll give you that."

"Well…" She pulls away, and I feel a sharp loss at the absence of her touch. "It's my job to be observant."

"Mine too." We're both observant, but not enough to get past this tension that has kept us at odds for years. If she could only see how much I want her, how much I love her.

Just tell her. Do it.

Marcy stands and stretches. "Well, I should get home. Long day tomorrow."

"It's Saturday." I walk her to the door.

"Yeah, but stylists don't run normal schedules like the rest of the world."

"You mean like doctors?" I chuckle. "I work tomorrow too."

"Day shift?"

"Yup."

Her smile warms me. "Well, don't work too hard."

"You too, Marcy." I open the door for her. "Be safe."

"I'm always safe, Rob." She waves as she walks down the hall. "Later!"

I close the door and Tabby appears at my feet. Scooping her into my arms, I return to the living room and clean up the remains of our meal.

If someone had told me Marcy and I would be sitting around like old friends, laughing and joking, I would have called them crazy.

But I like it. It gives me hope there could be something more between us.

I just wish I had the courage to tell her how I feel.

Chapter Eleven
Marcy

What the hell am I doing?

I twirl the card for the Plaza Hotel between my fingers. There's a room number scrawled on the back. Fuck. I can't seriously be considering this. Can I?

After the impromptu dinner with Rob last night, nothing has eased the ache—not cold showers, not self-stimulation. I should have been honest with him, but I couldn't do it. Whatever tenuous friendship we've formed over the past few weeks is hanging precariously by a thread. I don't want to ruin it by throwing myself at him.

No. I need to distract myself. Maybe have a little fun. Work has been stressful, and between the wedding and Rob's strange behavior, I deserve a break from the usual.

By break, I didn't mean to disregard my *no dating clients* rule. But Vic seemed sincere enough when he issued the invitation earlier this week. It's just dinner. Right?

I pick up the phone and punch in the digits for the hotel. When the front desk clerk answers, I request Vic's room.

"Hello?"

"It's Marcy, the stylist." I lick my lips, and my heart pounds like a drum in a cave.

"You changed your mind?"

"Maybe." I twist the cord around my fingers. "You want to grab dinner?"

"I could eat. The restaurant in the hotel is fantastic. Meet you there at seven?"

"Perfect." I hang up the phone and nearly drift off into space.

This is the craziest thing I've done in a while. It's been too long since I've had any kind of action. The last guy wasn't even worth the effort. Such a disappointment. The guy I want is the one I can't have. There's no Rob tonight. It's just Vic and me. Whatever happens, happens. I'm not going to stress about it.

After an hour of primping and prepping, I manage to nail that effortless, not-trying-too-hard glam I see so many women wasting hours to perfect. Looking good is my brand. I need to stay on top of it. I pop in a stick of Doublemint gum and slip on my glasses.

I manage to flag down a cab and take it to the Plaza. Inside, the concierge points me toward the hotel restaurant. Shit, this place is high-class. I tug at my skirt, knowing I must look like I'm in the wrong place. Screw it. I straighten up as I enter the restaurant.

Vic stands when he sees me. "You look lovely."

"Thank you." I warm at the compliment and take the seat across from him.

"Would you like something to drink?" Vic waves to the waiter.

"Red wine, please." I address the waiter before turning back to Vic.

He's wearing a blue-and-red pinstripe button-down dress shirt and black trousers. It's simple, but the color amplifies his eyes. He's handsome. Definitely movie-star quality handsome. And charming to a fault.

Guilt creeps in. Why should I feel guilty? He asked me to join him for dinner, and damn it, I'm going to soak up the attention.

I scan the menu and steal a glance at him over the top. "So how's the promo tour for the new movie going?"

"Great. We have a few more interviews here next week before flying to LA for the red-carpet event." Vic's gaze lingers on me as he reaches for his glass of water. "Perhaps I could entice you to be my date for opening night."

It takes me two whole seconds before the implication of his words sinks into my addled brain. "We haven't even gotten through dinner and you're inviting me to LA for a massive, highly televised event?"

"I have a good feeling about you." He winks.

The waiter returns with my wine and takes our orders.

Once he leaves, Vic leans closer. "So tell me about yourself. How did you become such a gifted stylist?"

Typically, I don't mind talking about my business, but this feels personal, intrusive, like he's asking about my private life rather than my professional skillset. I can't form a realistic response so I take a sip of my wine, giving myself time to figure out what I can offer without revealing too much.

"Well, my grandmother taught me to sew when I was a teenager." I spin a yarn a mile long, hoping he'll eat it up. There are nuggets of truth woven through the story, but nothing that could be traced to my broken past. I might be outlandish in my clothes and personality, but I prefer to keep my past buried and locked away from prying eyes. I'm not one for wearing my shame in public for sympathy or ridicule.

The more I speak, the more he listens. It's like he's absorbing all of the information, and I can't help but wonder if he's interested or just placating me. Finally, I shift the conversation to him.

"Enough about me, tell me about you." I smile and sip my wine. "Did you always want to be an actor?"

"No. I kinda fell into it." He rakes his fingers through his hair and chuckles. "I was working construction on a film set when the lead actor was injured trying to do a stunt. I stepped in for the stunt work. After that gig, the director called me to audition for a role in his new film." Vic shrugs. "I fell in love with it."

"That's wonderful. It's a relief when you love your job. I mean, I couldn't imagine doing a job I hate." I shiver at the thought of being stuck in a thankless job I didn't enjoy, and I'm reminded how fortunate I am for all I have.

Dinner arrives, and we eat while enjoying conversation scattered throughout the meal. Being in his company is the reprieve I need. His presence garners looks from neighboring tables, but he's kind and gracious to those who recognize him.

Vic Simmons is an enigma, and I find myself wanting to know more about him.

But that's not how this works. I only accepted his invitation because I knew there could be nothing between us. Just distraction and maybe some hot sex.

After dessert, a decadent crème brulee, Vic signs the check and meets my gaze. "Shall we?" He stands and offers his hand.

I take it and let him escort me from the restaurant. I feel like a celebrity myself as we weave through the tables to the exit.

In the corridor, he leans down. "Would you like to come up to my room?" He whispers the question against my ear.

"That depends on what you have planned?" I tease, brushing against his body with my own.

"I have every intention of seeing those lips put to good use." His blue eyes blaze with heat and unspoken promises.

But there's something beneath it. Something dark and unnerving. A warning to walk away.

"Mmm. Tempting, but maybe another night." I pull my hand free.

In a flash, the blue in his eyes turns to a raging, stormy gray. He snatches me by the wrist and pulls me into an alcove leading to the bathrooms. I try to wrench my hand from his grip, but he's too strong. My heels twist uselessly on the carpet as I try to catch my balance, stumbling behind him.

"Vic!"

He smothers my shout with his mouth as he pins me against the wall. We're alone in the dark hallway. I push against his chest, but he doesn't budge. His hot, unwelcome kiss leaves me stunned, and I squeal in protest when he shoves his tongue between my lips. He steals my breath, plunders my mouth.

The roast chicken I had for dinner churns in my stomach. No matter how hard I shove against his body, he doesn't move. He's a brick wall of solid muscle and determination.

Help! I'm screaming in my head, but no one can hear me. I have to get him off me before I choke on the panic.

In desperation, I bite his tongue. He rears back and glares at me. There's a flash of movement and a burst of pain as his hand connects with the side of my face. Warmth blooms across my face.

I gasp and clutch my cheek. It's wet. He strikes a second time, sending me reeling. Then he grasps my shoulders and slams me against the wall.

My skin burns and my brain shorts out.

It's not Vic, it's Dan. He's standing over me with a wooden rolling pin. I barely scream when he swings it at me. My body aches from the countless strikes. I sob and pull inside myself, covering my head with my hands, hiding my face. *Stop!* I scream, but he doesn't listen. He keeps going until he's content with the damage.

Just like that, Dan is gone and Vic is back.

"You'd best not decline such a gracious invitation." He grits his teeth.

No, I can't let him win. I won't let him best me like Dan did. I'm stronger now. Stronger than I was. I can fight back.

With all the determination I possess, I tip my head back and meet his gaze. I spit in his face.

"You'll pay for that, bitch." He draws his arm back to strike me again. A shadow appears at the end of the hallway.

Thank God! Before I can shout for help, Vic drops his hand over my mouth.

"Ah-ah. Before you scream for help, consider your business. Your passion." His breath against my skin makes me gag. "It would be a shame for you to lose such a prestigious connection." He sneers. "No one will believe you anyway."

Vic drops his hand and walks away, leaving me alone in the hall. I manage to stumble into the bathroom and lock the door. My heart's racing and my legs feel like they're about to give out. But I can't stay here. I need to get home. I need…

Fuck.

One glance in the mirror tells me exactly what I need: a doctor.

There's blood smearing my face. I manage to clean it the best I can and find the cut. With a paper towel pressed to my cheek, I manage to keep a low profile during my escape from the hotel.

The cabbie doesn't spare me a second look when I climb into his car. I pay him extra not to ask questions and get me home quickly.

Inside the safety of my apartment, my composure shatters. I crumple to the floor in a broken heap. Dragging myself across the floor, I slowly progress to the phone by the couch.

I dial the number I know by heart. The line is picked up.

"Hello?"

The quiet sobs transform into heart-wrenching gulps of air as the panic and pain coalesce inside me.

"Marcy?" Rob's voice echoes in my ear, and relief fills me.

"Help me." I hiccup. "Please."

"Fuck. Where are you?"

"Home. Hurry." I disconnect the phone and curl up in a ball as the emotions consume me.

I knew better. I fucking knew better than to trust him.

And now I'm right back where I started all those years ago.

CHAPTER TWELVE
ROB

The heart-wrenching sobs echo through the line.

Help me. Please.

The moment I hear those words, I reach for my shoes. All the air disappears from my lungs as my world is ripped out from under me.

Hurry.

"Fuck." I race down to my apartment and grab my medical bag. Within five minutes, I'm in a cab, racing downtown.

The drive is torment, but I shove aside my impatience. I can't get to her faster by foot or subway. By the time I reach her place, it's nearly midnight. Panic infuses me.

What the hell happened? Why was she in tears? The last time I heard her in such a state was the night she left her ex. The night I stitched her wounds and bit back my fury.

I felt a shift last night during our friendly dinner. The soft transition from tolerating someone's presence to friendship. I shouldn't hope for much, but knowing she called me for help instead of one of her other friends leaves me certain there's something more.

Then again, she called her brother's number. I just happened to be there to answer the phone. Maybe she was reacting out of desperation, out of survival, calling the one person she could trust. Her brother.

But he's not here. I am. I answered the phone. I heard her sobs, her plea for help.

The uncertainty mixes with the adrenaline coursing through my system. I need to see her. I need to be sure she's okay. Fear pulses through me, hot and suffocating. I urge the driver to speed up, tell him it's an emergency.

Because it is.

When the taxi driver pulls up outside her building, I toss some bills at him and dart from the cab. A quick glance down the alley reveals her bedroom light glowing like a beacon. The curtain sways in the faint breeze, and I catch a glimpse of her shadow beyond the fire escape that crisscrosses the side of the building.

She must have stepped outside for a smoke.

I slip past a couple exiting the building and head inside. When I reach her door, I'm breathless, and my pounding heart echoes in my chest like a jackhammer.

"Marcy." I pound my fist on the door. "It's Rob. Open the door, baby."

My hand flexes impatiently at the distinct sound of the deadbolt and chain. When the door opens, it's like someone's taken a sucker punch straight to my solar plexus. Rage, red hot and all-consuming, floods me.

"What the hell happened, Marcy?" I rush inside and close the door behind me, then lock it. My gaze never strays from her.

Her eyes are red and swollen from crying. But it's not the tears that have me fuming. It's the darkening bruise framing her face and the gash high on her cheek, leaving a trail of blood against her pale skin. She presses a bloodstained rag to it and the tears flow anew.

Without thought, I pull her into my arms. Her shoulders tremble as I hold her close. She sobs against my chest, and I let her.

A million thoughts slam into me at once. Was she attacked on the street? Did someone mug her? I hold my tongue. I'll have to wait for answers. Right now, she just needs to be held. To know she's safe.

"It's all right, baby." I rub my hands gently across her back in a soothing rhythm. "You're safe now. It's over." I repeat it, over and over, until she quiets in my embrace and the trembling dissipates to soft hiccups.

When she finally pulls away, she groans at the sight of her blood on my shirt. "Sorry." Marcy sniffs.

"I work in the ER. Bloodstains might be a bitch to get out of my lab coat, but they don't scare me." I offer a smile and guide her to the couch. "Sit down. Let me take a look."

Marcy sits beside me, her gaze fixed on the floor. I put my bag on the coffee table before turning toward her.

"Chin up. Let me see."

She drops the bloody rag into her lap. I gently cup her chin in my hand and rotate her face in the light. Contusion on both sides with bruising. A laceration in the soft tissue across her zygomatic arch. It's not deep, but it's still bleeding. Damn it.

I reach into the kit and withdraw antiseptic and some cotton swabs. I'll clean it, then put some ice on the swelling. Hopefully, it'll stop the bleeding as well.

"It'll sting." I dab antiseptic on the wound, and she flinches, hissing in a breath. "Sorry."

I take the rag from her hand and place her fingers on the cotton ball against the wound. "Hold this. I'll get some ice."

In the freezer, I find a frozen bag of peas. That'll work. My mind races as the onslaught of emotions propels me to action. Even though I want to push for details, I don't. I grab a clean hand towel from the closet and wrap the peas before replacing the cotton with the cold pack. Years of training kick in, and I walk through the motions to ensure she's cared for properly.

"This should calm things down," I assure her, but she still won't meet my gaze. She's withdrawn due to the trauma.

I sigh. "Marcy. Look at me."

Those bewitching eyes, full of pain and shame, finally meet mine. Her lower lip trembles.

"What happened?" My breath catches in my throat at the way she cringes at the question.

"Don't. I can't, he'll…" She bites her lip and shakes her head. "Don't ask."

"He?" The barely suppressed rage boils to the surface. "Who did this to you, Marcy?" I grit my teeth, trying like hell not to snap in half from the pressure building inside me.

She shakes her head harder. "I can't."

The normally tough-as-nails woman I've loved for years sits

before me like she had that horrible night. Fragile and bruised, fearful and angry. But this time, there's more. She's embarrassed about it. There's a layer of shame across the surface.

"Who are you protecting?" I ask, my voice stern.

"I'm not protecting anyone!" she snaps.

In that moment, I see the fire ignite in her eyes once more. There's the fighter I know and love.

"Fine." I lift my hands in surrender, but I remain steadfast beside her. "Do you have any other injuries? Ribs, arms, legs, abdomen? Any discomfort?"

"No." She shifts the peas away from her cheek, and the cold has staunched the bleeding to a drop or two.

"Why didn't you just go to the ER?" I open the pill canister and pour two ibuprofen into my palm.

"Because I didn't want anyone asking stupid questions." Her strength must be returning if the forcefulness of her responses is any indicator. She takes the pills and pops them without water. "It's not a big deal."

"Bullshit, Marcy. You called your brother's penthouse in tears, barely able to get the words out."

"I panicked. I needed…" Her voice falters. "I forgot he wasn't home."

"But I answered." I nod with painful understanding. "You weren't calling for me."

"I was."

Her soft response leaves me stunned.

"You helped me just as much as Arthur did that night. I'm glad you answered the phone. I didn't have your number."

My heart can't take the goddamned roller coaster much longer. I can't care for her unless she wants me to, but she won't tell me what happened. And I'm afraid if I pry, she'll push me away again.

"Marcy, I want to help you. But if you don't tell me what happened, my hands are tied."

"I made a mistake." Her jaw clenches. "I trusted someone I shouldn't have, and this is what I get." Her lip quivers again, but judging by the steely glint in her eyes, this time it's from fury, not fear. "I shouldn't have gone, but I did. There's nothing I can do about it now."

"You went out on a date?" Disbelief mingles with the anguish churning in my gut. Once the realization settles, the rage ignites like an inferno. "He fucking hit you."

"It was just dinner. But he wanted more than that." Her gaze settles on the far wall. "I told him no. He wasn't pleased with my response."

"Fuck, Marcy." I spit the words out not realizing how they'll affect her. She flinches. "Sorry." The emotions rise to a rolling boil. "Did anyone see him hit you?"

"No." Her hand is shaking where it presses the cold pack to her cheek. "But someone walked past, and I was able to get away from him before he could do worse."

"Tell me who he is, Marcy," I plead. "Tell me, and I'll make sure that bastard never walks again. Never touches another woman. Never knows another moment of pleasure in his miserable life."

A hint of a smile touches her lips. But it's sad and lost in painful memories. "I can't, Rob. Please. I know you want to help me…" Her words trail off, and she shrugs.

Resigned, I put my kit back in the bag and close it. "Well, make sure you rest. I'll check on you tomorrow."

I stand, and her hand grabs my wrist. "Please stay, Rob." Fear reflects in her eyes again. "I don't want to be alone tonight."

Damn it.

I exhale sharply, praying for strength. Of all the nights for her to invite me to stay…and not for the reason I want her to ask me to stay. I must have been a goddamned saint in a prior life.

"Okay. I'll stay." I place the bag on the table. "Come on, let's get you to bed."

She leads the way, and I place a butterfly bandage on the cut before I put a larger bandage over that. She doesn't need to wake up with a blood-soaked pillow if it bleeds during the night.

I pull the sheet over her. A gentle breeze drifts in from the cracked window. It's warm tonight, so I turn on the fan. The rhythmic noise lulls her.

"Goodnight, Marcy."

"Night, Rob." She closes her eyes. "Thank you."

I nod, but she's already dozing. I bend down and kiss her forehead. The scent of her sweet shampoo lingers in my nose as I retreat to the living room and crash on the couch. I punch the throw pillow and lay my head on it, staring at the dark ceiling.

Yeah, I'm a goddamned saint. But at least I'm doing what I've always wanted to do, what I should have been doing from the start.

Keeping her safe.

CHAPTER THIRTEEN
MARCY

He's chasing me. The hallway stretches out before me, an endless tunnel leading into darkness. My screams evaporate in the void.

He snatches my hair and pulls me back to him. There's no escape.

I claw at his arms, his chest, his face, but nothing stops him. He sneers as he shoves me against the wall and rips my clothes.

When I fight him, he beats me into submission.

Exhausted, I'm naked and bleeding. He unbuckles his belt and reaches into his pants. I cringe, tightly closing my eyes.

No, no, no! This isn't happening. It's not real. The light streams across his face.

Rob?

I jerk awake. Sweat coats my skin. I'm wearing my pajamas, tucked into my own bed. Slowly my gaze focuses in the darkness. What a fucking dream. I wipe my brow and freeze when I see shadows shift in the far corner of the room. Even the blood in my veins stops flowing.

Someone's in the room with me.

"Rob?" I hazard the word, but it's not him.

A figure materializes in the darkness. The light from outside amplifies the shadow on the wall. The dream returns with a vengeance, gripping me by the throat and shaking me.

A scream wrenches free.

The shadowed figure bolts across my bedroom toward the open window. When they pass the door, it flies open, colliding with the intruder.

"Marcy." Rob flicks on the light switch. He's shirtless and has a frying pan in his hand. Eyes wild, he scans the room.

The dark figure groans in a heap on the floor. Rob reaches down and snatches them by the arm, dragging them to their feet.

Black leggings, black shirt, and black domino mask.

What the fuck? A burglar? The fear slowly dissolves at the reveal of the intruder. They attempt to pull away from Rob, but he tightens his grip.

"You're hurting me," the burglar cries out, pulling against his hold.

"A woman?" I gape at her and untangle myself from the sheet.

"Let me go." The woman sidesteps me when I reach for her mask.

"Knock it off." Rob gives her a firm shake.

I pull off the mask and the cap holding her hair in place. A mess of frizzy, dark red curls tumbles free, framing a pair of wide green eyes. She could be a model if the industry weren't hellbent on every woman being a size two. In the light, her generous curves fill out the black ensemble.

Any other day, I'd say she was a knockout, but not here, not now. She broke into my fucking apartment.

"Well, well, looks like we caught ourselves a cat burglar." Rob grins as he drags the woman into the living room.

I follow behind and retrieve a carving knife from the kitchen. Better safe than sorry.

Rob shoves the woman onto the couch and points the frying pan at her. "Don't move."

With his attention still focused on her, Rob picks up the phone. He struggles to dial the number. "Watch her, Marcy. If she tries to run, aim for her throat."

The woman's eyes widen. Her gaze shifts to me, and I recognize the fear hiding there, just beneath the surface. The adrenaline drains from my body, replaced immediately with fury.

"Why the hell did you break into my apartment?" I hiss at her. "I don't have anything worth stealing."

The cat burglar cocks her head and studies me, but she says nothing.

"Richards, it's Thompson. I need you to give me a hand with something." Rob glances at me, irritation on his brow. "Yes, I realize it's four in the morning." He sighs. "No, this can't wait."

Who in the world did he call? I keep my focus on the

intruder, who seems as invested in Rob's conversation as I am.

"I'm at a friend's place, and we've had a break-in." Rob taps the pan against his thigh, and I'm drawn to the way his shoulder muscles flex beneath his skin. "No, I can't call the cops." He looks at the ceiling. "It's complicated. Look you're going to have to trust me. Get your ass over here." He rattles off the address and hangs up the phone.

"Who was that?" I ask when he turns toward us.

"Just a friend." He sits on the coffee table across from our uninvited guest. "A detective. He owes me a favor."

The intruder's mouth gapes. "You're not calling the cops?"

Rob snorts. "Trust me. When Richards gets ahold of you, you're going to wish I had called the cops."

"Is that the guy my brother knows down at the precinct? The one you—"

"Yeah, he's the cop I saved the night Arthur and I went club-hopping after graduation." Rob shakes his head. "He made detective a few years ago."

"I didn't realize you were still friends with him." I sit on the arm of the chair.

The woman shifts uncomfortably when she sees a glint of the blade in my hand, and her gaze shifts to Rob. Once the detective shows up and takes her off our hands, she'll be a distant memory. I'm not even paying attention to her anymore.

No, it's Rob's half-naked form driving me to distraction. And it seems the woman in black is having the same problem. Hunger fills her bright eyes. I want to claw them out of her head.

"Yeah, we get together at the bar for drinks once a month. I've worked with him on cases before too." Rob's response pulls me from my fantasies.

"So what do we do with her until he arrives?" I glare at the intruder who's drinking in every inch of Rob's bare skin.

"Just sit tight. He said he'd be here in twenty."

"Could you at least cover yourself? She looks like she's about to eat you alive." I grab his shirt from the chair behind me and toss it at him.

Rob chuckles and pulls on the shirt.

The cat burglar pouts. "Spoilsport."

"You shouldn't even be talking. Felon. You broke into *my* apartment, remember?" I jab the knife toward her.

Gently, Rob pries the blade from my hand and sets it beside him. "I don't feel like filing a police report tonight just because you were jealous."

I barely register his comment before the intruder protests.

"What? You mean you were bluffing about the knife to the throat?" She huffs.

"*I* was." Rob jabs his thumb at me. "But I don't think she would have hesitated to slit your throat. You're not exactly an innocent bystander here." He sobers and leans closer. "What the hell were you thinking?"

She shrugs and tosses him a saucy wink. "I was thinking I'd get lucky."

Red fills my vision. I'm about to rip this girl to pieces. Her cute nose, those sensual curves, her intoxicating eyes. She knows exactly what she's doing. Trying to throw herself on Rob's mercy.

Over my dead fucking body.

"Sorry, sweetheart. You're not my type." Rob leans back and shakes his head. "Besides, breaking and entering isn't exactly a romantic way to meet someone."

"Your loss, honey."

I can't take any more of this bitch. I'm going to do something drastic if I don't get some air. I shoot to my feet and stomp to the bathroom. Inside, I splash some water on the unbandaged side of my face and dab it with a towel. My whole face pulses with a bone-deep ache.

The bruises are starting to appear beneath the skin. It'll take heavy concealer to hide this shit from my clients, but I'll manage. Big sunglasses and a wide-brimmed hat does wonders for curious onlookers too. Hell, if it works for celebs, it'll work for me.

After using the toilet, I stop in my bedroom and lean out the open window. Yup, the fire escape ladder has been lowered. Bitch must be a damned spider monkey. I retreat into the room and close the window, ensuring I lock it. It's too hot to sleep with the windows closed. Guess I'll have to figure out another way to keep cool this summer…or splurge on an AC unit.

A knock at the door pulls me from my thoughts. I dash into the living room and wave to Rob. "I got it."

Peering through the peephole, I see a tall, somber man with a day's worth of scruff on his jaw and a scowl deep in his brow. I unlock the door and open it.

"Ma'am." He nods in respect, but I note his long perusal of my face. My hand covers the bandage protectively. "I'm looking for Dr. Thompson."

"He's in here. Please, come in." I step aside and allow him entry.

"Thanks for coming." Rob rises to his feet and extends his hand.

"This better be worth dragging my ass out of bed, Thompson." He glowers at Rob. "What the hell is going on?"

Rob gestures to me, encouraging me to tell him what happened.

"Well, I woke up and found this burglar in my bedroom looking through my things." I point to the woman seated on the couch.

My nerves are exposed, frayed, sparking like live wires of electricity. It feels like one more thing heaped on top of everything else. I'm about to scream into the sun.

"Did she do this?" He massages his own cheek with a fingertip, referring to my injury.

"No. Different incident." I fold my arms across my chest.

"Okay." His gaze narrows before shifting to the intruder. "And why didn't you just call the department?"

"I don't want a whole bunch of questions and paperwork right now," Rob says, his voice low. "I'm sure you can talk some sense into our…guest here."

A grin splits the detective's lips. He's handsome in that rough and tumble, brash, hard-boiled detective way. Dark hair, dark eyes, an even darker soul. This man has seen some shit. I shiver at the thought, even though my skin is overheated from the stale air in the room.

"I'll take care of her." The detective reaches down and grabs her arm, pulling her from the couch.

"Wait, don't let him take me! Call the cops. But don't let him take me. Please." Panic fills her eyes. "Please," she begs as he drags her toward the door.

"It's too late, kid. You're my problem now."

He pauses at the door and murmurs something in her ear. She stills immediately, her mouth pressed in a thin line.

"Thanks, Richards." Rob waves. "See you next week."

"Yeah, yeah." He nods to me. "Good night, ma'am."

"Night."

I lock the door behind them. Relief fills me at their absence.

Rob returns the frying pan and knife to the kitchen. "Good thing you told me to stay." He grins. "You might have killed someone tonight."

Irritation floods me. How can he tease me at a time like this? My emotions are all over the damn place. After the incident with Vic and now this burglar, I don't think I'll be able to sleep for a month. At least.

"Fuck you, Rob." I stomp past him, determined just to be out of his insufferable presence.

"Whoa." He grabs me by the hand. "Stop. Hold on."

I can't face him. Tension pulses between us. His hand burns like a brand against my skin. My body tenses when he steps closer. I pinch my eyes closed and take several deep breaths.

If I do this, if I face him now, my restraint will snap.

"Look at me, Marcy." I can feel his fingertips against my chin.

No. No. No. Don't do it. Fight against it. Don't say or do something you'll regret.

"Please, baby."

His plea breaks me.

CHAPTER FOURTEEN
ROB

I fucked it up again. Damn it.

I meant it as a joke, something to lighten the mood. But instead of easing the tension, it inflamed her temper. There were a hundred things I could have said to offer comfort and support, but I stuck my foot in my mouth instead.

Her pulse pounds beneath my fingertips pressed against her wrist. My other hand lingers on her jaw, and I plead for her to look at me. A smart man would let her go, let her be angry at him. But I can't bear the thought that I caused her even a moment's pain.

Marcy spins around, pulling away from my touch. Her eyes blaze with internal fire.

"You're right. I almost killed someone tonight. Is there anything else you'd like to point out?" She folds her arms across her chest, emphasizing her breasts hidden by the thin tank top.

"Marcy, I didn't…"

"Didn't what? Think before you spoke? No shit." She huffs and throws her hands up. "Thank you for coming to my rescue tonight. Now get the fuck out."

One step forward and two steps back. My hope deflates at her dismissal, but I've gained this ground, and I refuse to give it up so easily. "I'm not leaving until you tell me what the fuck just happened?"

"What happened?" She scoffs. "That bitch happened. Breaking into my house is one thing but throwing herself all over you to try to get out of any punishment is a whole new low."

I blink twice. She's actually jealous. The realization strikes me like a physical blow and leaves me reeling.

But this is progress. I've never seen her truly jealous before. The flush of pink on her skin, the flaring nostrils, the firm set of her lips. She's livid, and now I know why.

"Wait a minute, are you telling me you're more upset because a woman flirted with me than you are that she broke into your apartment and scared the hell out of you?"

"No." She stiffens at the accusation, but it's too late. I see the truth through the cracks of her facade.

"I've known you for too long, Marcy, and I can read you like a book." A smile tugs at my lips, but I force myself to suppress it. I'll have the truth from her if it kills me.

"No, you can't."

"I can." I step closer, and she backs away from me, eyes wide. "What? Are you afraid I might take her up on her unspoken offer?"

"No."

"Wrap my hand in those curls and pin her against the wall. Take my fill of those lips and her dangerous curves." Satisfaction pours through me at her indignant gasp.

"I don't care what you do or with whom." She jabs her finger in my chest right before she hits the wall. "But I'll be damned if I let you screw some hussy in my living room."

My hands rest on the wall, framing her shoulders, holding her in place. Her quick breaths amplify the rise and fall of her chest. My gaze dips to the creamy skin exposed by the gaping tank top.

Enough games. I'm tired of denying the truth. I want Marcy, but she needs to know exactly how I feel first.

"So that's how it goes, huh? You're allowed to criticize my choices, but I can't ask you about your date."

She shivers when my words strike true.

"I'm only good enough when you go out with some asshole and he gets rough. Then you call me to patch you up."

"No." She shakes her head, and her scent surrounds me. It drives me wild.

"Is that all I am to you? A bleeding heart with a medical degree who's got a soft spot for his best friend's sister?"

Her mouth drops open. "I have never taken advantage of your kindness or your friendship with my brother."

"Not knowingly, perhaps." I lick my lips and hold her gaze steadily. "But you have to know, after all these years, I don't care solely because you're Arthur's little sister."

"What?" Her slow blink confirms the realization sinking into her brain. "I don't understand."

"I've wanted you since the first day we met." My heartbeat thunders in my chest in an arrhythmia. I might be dying, but I don't care. I've waited years to say this.

"But…" She shakes her head. "Why tell me now?"

"There's never been a good moment. Until now." I exhale a breath lodged in my chest. "I want you, Marcy. I've always wanted you."

Those luminous eyes hold mine for what feels like eternity. Marcy grabs my tee shirt and pulls me down to her level.

Her mouth is on mine in an instant, hot and sweet. She kisses me hard and fast.

Suddenly, I'm pulled into a vortex of pleasure, and I surrender completely.

I moan as the final piece of my restraint falls away. My hands drop to her shoulders and pull her close. My mouth opens beneath hers.

I'm lost in the kiss. In her. She tastes like pure bliss. I'm as close to heaven as I'll ever get.

Her arms encircle my neck, and I lift her off the ground, pinning her to the wall. Those slender legs wrap around me, and she grinds her hips against mine. I hiss at the pressure of her heat rocking against my aching cock.

Fuck. I need to be inside her.

I stumble back and carry her to the couch. When I sit, she comes with me, straddling my thighs.

I've fantasized about this for so long, it feels like a dream. Like she'll vanish in a plume of smoke.

I softly cup her injured cheek in my hand, and she draws back. Her eyes are glazed with passion and desperation.

"Are you sure you want this?"

"Rob, I swear to God, if you don't fuck me now, I'll spontaneously combust." She pulls her tank top over her head and tosses it to the floor.

I suck in a breath, and my hand slides up over her side. I take one breast in my hand. It overflows, and I squeeze, drawing a guttural moan from deep in her throat. She grinds her hips against me.

"Condom?" she whispers in my ear while her hands unfasten my belt.

"I don't…have any." Regret fills me. I know better than to take the chance, but I'm desperate. Reason breaks through. "I'm sorry. I'll…"

"When was the last time?" She nips my earlobe and tugs my pants down my hips.

"Years. Fuck. It's been years."

Marcy slides off my lap, pulling my pants to my ankles. She kneels and removes them completely. Her thumbs hook in the waistband of her shorts, and as she stands, she draws them down.

The sight of the curls between her thighs leaves me ravenous. I snatch her by the waist and pull her back into my lap.

She collides with me, and my cock brushes against her slick center.

"You?" The question is more of a gasp than a word.

I'm two seconds from taking her hard and fast. But I won't…not if she doesn't want me to. My restraint is hanging by a fraying thread.

"Too fucking long." She whimpers when I rock my hips against hers. "Rob, I need you. Now."

"But…"

"On the pill." Marcy grasps my jaw in her hand and kisses me hard. "Make me come."

My body responds immediately to her command. I lift her hips and position her over my cock. She sinks down, and I watch with fascination as she takes me.

Her eyes flutter closed, her nails dig into my shoulders. The heat of her surrounds me, clenching tight around my cock.

Once she's taken all of me, I take three deep breaths to keep myself from coming on the spot. My hands grip her hips to keep her from moving, and I rest my head on her chest.

Her fingers thread in my hair, and her laugh rumbles through me. I tease her nipple with my teeth, coaxing a moan from her wicked mouth.

Marcy bucks against me, and my cock swells even more.

"I won't last if you keep that up."

"We have all night," she croons in my ear as she gently rocks back and forth.

"Fuck it." Gripping her waist, I thrust deep.

She gasps and holds tight as we fall into a rhythm. I'm drowning in sensations of her, trying to hold out until she takes her own pleasure.

"That's it, baby." I urge her on as her soft moans fill the space between us. "Take what you need."

This unleashes something within her. Gone is the hesitancy. The restraint. She holds tight as she grinds her hips, searching for friction and pressure. I slide my thumb over her clit and circle it in time with her panting gasps. Her head falls back in surrender.

I've never seen anything more beautiful in my life. A goddess taking her pleasure, eyes closed, mouth parted. Her whimpers tell me she's close to orgasm. When she finally breaks, it's my name on her lips that tips me over the edge.

I come hard, filling her. Her pussy clenches around me with the aftershocks of her climax, milking every ounce of pleasure from my body.

Fuck. Me.

When she collapses against me, we cling to each other, covered in sweat. It's not how I imagined it. It's so much better.

I stroke my hand over her spine and she moans, arching deeper against me. "Shower?"

"Hmm?"

"Shower. To cool off."

"That sounds amazing." Marcy kisses me. Slow and drugging. My cock twitches inside her. She laughs. "Ready again so soon?"

"What can I say? I'm making up for lost time."

We manage to disentangle ourselves and stumble into her small bathroom. I let her shower, and then step in behind her.

There's not nearly enough room to do what I want to do to her, so instead, I slide my fingers deep into her cunt.

Her lovely moans echo off the tile when she comes, soaking my fingers. I lick them clean, making her eyes widen. She's sweet. I can't wait to taste her again.

And again. And again.

Marcy is mine, and I'll be damned if I'm going to let her go now that I've finally claimed her.

CHAPTER FIFTEEN
MARCY

What is happening to me?

Every fantasy I ever had about Rob never came close to the reality. I don't know what finally snapped, but his confession should have left me reeling. Instead, relief flooded me.

I've wanted him for so long, actually having him is surreal. And when he let me take control on the couch? Fuck, that was the hottest thing he could have done. I don't think I've come that hard…ever.

"Bed, now," he whispers against my skin, gently nudging me out of the shower.

"You love giving orders, don't you?" I towel dry my torso and step aside, giving him room.

He cocks his head. "Sweetheart, I've wanted you in my bed for a long time. Now that I finally have you there, I intend to explore every inch of you with my mouth."

Gooseflesh pebbles my skin at the sinful promise. "My bed, you mean."

"Semantics." He gives my ass a playful swat. The sting warms me.

Rob is more adventurous than I ever imagined. Granted, I may have tried to downplay the possibility of him being a thoughtful lover to quell the need burning inside me.

The sun is rising, but I'm wide awake and desperate for Rob to make good on his promise. I toss the towel over the chair and sprawl on the bed like a starfish basking in the early morning light.

He watches from the doorway, towel slung low on his hips, damp hair hanging across his forehead. He pushes it back and stalks closer.

I never knew all those muscles were hidden beneath his

polos and scrubs. I want to trace my tongue over every ridge and leave my mark on that pristine skin.

Holding his gaze, I draw my leg up and let the warm air brush against my pussy. He pauses at the foot of the bed as if waiting for an invitation.

I draw my finger along my swollen lips. His eyes darken two shades while they follow my gentle strokes.

A growl rips from his throat as he climbs on the bed, settling between my thighs. He shoves my hand away and nudges my legs wider, exposing me. My breath catches when he blows across my aching clit. Then his mouth covers me, and I'm caught up in the storm once more.

While his tongue teases my folds, I run my fingers through his hair, gripping tight. He suckles my clit in his mouth. The sensation overwhelms me. I buck my hips, and he deepens his exploration, devouring my pussy with the same hunger he showed in his kiss. His moan sends shockwaves through my body.

Panting and gasping, I cling to him, unable to relieve the tension building inside me.

Rob lifts his gaze to meet mine. He's taking his time making good on his promise to explore every inch of me with his mouth.

When he finally slides two fingers in, rubbing with the perfect amount of pressure, I combust, my head falling back against the blankets.

"Fuck." My grip tightens as the orgasm hits. Sparks of pleasure radiate through me like fireworks against a black sky.

But Rob doesn't relent. He doubles his efforts and drinks me dry.

When I release him, he leans back and grins, his lips glistening with my arousal. He wipes his mouth with the back of his hand. That shouldn't be as hot as it is.

"I'm not done with you, sweetheart." He pulls my weightless body up and kisses me. "Put your hands on the wall."

I manage to shift my pleasure-wrought body to the head of the bed and place my palms against the headboard. Anticipation sparks like a live wire through my limbs.

Rob trails his hand along the inside of my thigh, nudging my legs wider. "Arch your back." I do as he instructs, and he groans in appreciation. "Good girl."

"Rob." His name falls from my lips when he trails his fingers over my pussy. "Please."

"Is this what you want, baby?" He slowly enters me from behind, and I'm drowning in him. With one arm around my waist, he encircles my throat with the other. "Keep your hands right there. Don't move."

The pressure of his arms is featherlight, but with his cock buried deep inside me, I'm grounded. My head spins. I've never been this vulnerable during sex, not since…

I pinch my eyes closed and tense at the unwelcome memory.

"Marcy," he whispers against my ear. "Breathe."

I exhale the breath I'd been holding, and Rob withdraws. He drives deep when I gasp. His teeth graze my shoulder, making me shiver as he pounds into me. Over and over, he takes control and pushes me higher. His hand presses on my lower abdomen, fingers skimming my sex.

The build is slower, more intimate, but Rob has me. Holds me close. His whispered endearments soothe me, his dirty words stoke the flame burning inside me.

I've never felt this before. This bond forged by pleasure and trust. I bask in it.

Rob pulls me away from the wall and lays me on the bed facing him. My pussy aches at the loss of his cock, but before I can protest, he's filling me again, deeper still.

His mouth covers mine, and I wrap my arms around him. The kiss consumes me.

My legs encircle his waist, and I ride the waves of pleasure, bucking my hips in tandem with his thrusts. I want all of him, every last drop of his being, bound to me.

Throughout years of longing, I feared I would never experience the passion I knew Rob possessed. I fought against it. Convinced myself he could never feel the same.

Lies. All of it. Why did I waste so much time?

Another orgasm crests, and Rob murmurs my name when

he follows with his own release. He rolls to his side and pulls me against him.

After a few quiet moments, Rob presses a kiss to my forehead. "Are you okay?"

"Never better." I nestle closer and drape myself across him. This I could get used to…the quiet moment of repose between bursts of pleasure. With Rob. Only with him.

He trails his finger across my bare arm. "You hungry?"

"Starving."

"I'll make you something." Rob kisses me softly on the lips and climbs out of bed.

I stretch across the mattress and watch him leave. Who has an ass like that? So squeezable.

Rob grabs his towel and turns, catching me red-handed. "Stop looking at me like I'm a piece of meat."

"What's good for the goose is good for the gander."

He huffs. "I've never looked at you like that."

"You just did. Right before you ate my pussy like a man starved."

"I did." He chuckles. "Fine. Stare all you want. I guess it's yours now anyway."

"Oh? So does that mean I can smack your ass in front of my brother?" I laugh at the look of horror on his face.

"Within reason, Marcy. Geezus, we're not animals in heat."

I crawl on all fours toward the end of the bed. "Speak for yourself."

"No." Rob holds his hand up, warding me off. "I'm making breakfast. Save that insatiable lust for later."

I pout, but the growling in my stomach agrees with Rob. "Fine."

Once Rob heads into the kitchen, I clean up in the bathroom and pull on a silk robe.

There's something so sexy about a man in an apron. Rob's donned my blue apron and has bacon sizzling in a skillet. He adds a little cream to the eggs before whisking.

"Smells delicious." I rest my cheek against his shoulder.

He kisses my forehead. "Grab a plate for the bacon."

I hold the plate as he places the bacon on it and drains some of the grease. When he pours the eggs into the skillet, I can't help but admire his fluid movements and his gracefulness in the kitchen.

Curiosity overwhelms me. "Do you like to cook?"

"I don't mind it." He smiles and it softens his features. "Don't really have a choice. I have to eat."

"Bachelor life can be rough."

He nods. "It's more fun to have someone to cook for."

I lean against the counter beside him. "Why didn't you ever marry?"

Rob's gaze fixes on me, honesty reflected in his handsome face. "Thought that would be obvious now."

My face warms when the realization hits me. "Marriage isn't all it's cracked up to be."

"With the wrong person, I agree. But with the right person..." He shrugs his shoulders, leaving the implication hanging in the air.

"Rob..."

"It's okay, Marcy. I understand." He pushes the egg around in the pan as it cooks. "You mind setting the table? Coffee should be ready."

Regret settles in the pit of my stomach. This wasn't how I wanted our morning to go. I have so many things I want to say, questions I want to ask, but suddenly, my brain doesn't want to cooperate. I set the table in silence and pour some coffee.

Rob puts the eggs on our plates and returns the skillet to the stovetop. I fidget with my fork until he joins me. Sitting at my small dining table like this seems even more intimate than the multiple rounds of sex we just enjoyed.

Breakfast in silence. I'm used to it when I'm alone, but with Rob's larger-than-life presence across from me, I can't focus on anything but him.

"Arthur and Kate will be home in a few days. I'm sure you're excited to see them." Rob sips his coffee.

"I am." I push the eggs around on my plate and take a halfhearted bite. "What do we tell them?"

"About us?" Rob arches his brow.

"Yeah."

"What do you want to tell them?"

"I don't know." I finish the last bite on my plate and shove it away.

"We don't have to tell them anything if you don't want to. Not until you're ready." Rob reaches across the table and takes my hand. "But I guarantee your brother will figure it out. He's not an idiot. He has eyes."

"Can we just enjoy the day together? Please? I don't want to worry about my brother or Kate or anything else." I drop my gaze to the table.

We should talk about us. What are *we* now? I can't bring myself to broach the topic knowing it'll make this all too real. If it's real, then it can end, and I can't handle that right now.

"Whatever you need, sweetheart."

Rob gives my hand one last squeeze before collecting the dishes and carrying them to the kitchen. We work as a team to clean up, and he wraps his arms around me when I finish the last dish.

His lips reignite that heat when he presses them to my neck. The hard press of his cock against my ass makes me wiggle my hips. He growls in response and tightens his grip on my waist.

"Come with me. I want to taste you again."

"No." I spin in his arms. "It's my turn to taste you."

Rob's eyes drift closed, and he murmurs a silent *thank you* to the heavens. I jab him in the ribs and laugh when he winces.

Caught up in the moment, he sweeps me into his arms and carries me into the bedroom. I spend the rest of the day exploring him as thoroughly as he explores me.

There's never been a more perfect day. Eat, sleep, fuck. With Rob, it's heaven. I never want it to end.

But when Monday morning comes, my alarm wakes me and the bed is empty. Was it just a dream?

There's a note on his pillow.

Marcy,

I left for work early. Didn't want to wake you. Had to go home and change. Working doubles all week. I'll call you when I have a free minute.

Love, Rob

I tuck the note into a book on my nightstand and manage to drag myself out of bed. My whole body burns with residual bliss at this recent adventure into sexual activity. I don't know how many times we had sex, but I'm not complaining. My body, however, is having second thoughts.

In the shower, my muscles relax under the spray. The note plays in my mind. I wish he would have woken me, but I understand. We both have jobs and lives. And they've intersected. What do we do now? Where do we go from here?

Part of me hopes I didn't fuck everything up by sleeping with Rob. I don't regret it—not even a little bit—but what the hell happens next?

What do I want?

This hasn't changed my mind on marriage. And Rob still deserves to have that option, should he desire a wife and a family. I'm just not sure it's something I might want in the future. Although, the thought of living with Rob has its appeal. We've been in each other's lives for so long, there's nothing about him I don't already know.

Then why the hell am I scared to death to tell him? To say the words?

What if he wants something totally different? I don't want to lose whatever this is.

But I know we'll have to talk it out at some point.

We'll both be busy all week. Maybe it'll give us both time to think things through. I just hope he doesn't start having second thoughts.

I just hope *I* don't start having second thoughts.

CHAPTER SIXTEEN
ROB

I haven't spoken to Marcy in two days. Not because I don't want to, but the ER has been chaos since Monday. Even Tabby has felt the brunt of my absence. Good thing Arthur and Kate returned from their honeymoon yesterday.

I spent the night at the hospital, curled up on a cot in one of the back rooms. We had two physicians call in this week, so I'm picking up the slack. I expected double shifts, but I didn't expect to move into the hospital permanently.

Thank God for Summer and the other nurses in the unit. They're more capable than some of the doctors on staff and give me a chance to breathe between cases. The stress of being on the floor has now overcome the adrenaline rush I used to get in my thirties. This shit is starting to take its toll on me. And now that Marcy and I are finally on the same page, a quiet life of office visits is starting to sound appealing. I've wasted too much time already; I'll be damned if I waste any more.

In my small office, I leaf through the files on my desk. These cases need notes. I glance at the phone. Maybe I should call her. It's two in the afternoon, and I'm pretty sure she's at work. I have the evening off, so I'll call her tonight when I'm home. Maybe we can grab some dinner.

Refocusing my wandering thoughts, I open the first file. The phone rings.

"Dr. Thompson." I lean it against my shoulder and finish a note in the patient's file.

"Rob, it's Arthur. Am I interrupting?"

I toss the pen aside. "No. What do you need?"

"Kate wants to know if you're free for dinner. She's making lasagna with a recipe she got in Italy. A thank you for watching Tabby."

My stomach growls at the thought of a home-cooked meal. I've eaten cafeteria food for the past few days, and my body will revolt if I imbibe one more gelatin bowl or chocolate pudding. As much as I don't want to intrude, this reprieve is exactly what I need. I can't help but wonder if Marcy will be there too.

"Yeah, my shift ends at six." I glance at the clock. Only four more hours.

"Perfect. Dinner will be ready at seven. See you then."

"Thanks." I hang up the phone and return to the stack of files.

As if the universe could sense my anticipation, it throws everything at me at once. Three traumas from a car accident, a sprained ankle, two screaming toddlers, and a very irritable octogenarian who has no interest in cooperating with the nurses round out my afternoon in the ER.

Exhausted, I manage to leave the hospital at six thirty. It takes me thirty minutes in traffic to get home, ten to shower, and five to pull on some clean clothes. God, I hope they're clean. When did I last do laundry? I really need to spend some time getting my place in order. The days swarm together, but all I can think about is Marcy.

It's quarter after seven when I knock on Arthur's door. Kate answers it.

"We were getting worried." She steps aside and lets me in.

"Yeah, sorry. Work was chaotic today." I hand her a bouquet of flowers I had picked up from a corner vendor on the way home. "How was Italy?"

Kate's cheeks pinken, and her eyes glaze over in that nostalgic way people get when remembering a happy memory. "It was heavenly."

Tabby weaves through my legs and mews. I pick her up and scratch her ears. "I'm glad you had a great time."

The scent of tomatoes, rosemary, and meat fills the air. My stomach growls. Kate takes Tabby from my arms when Arthur appears.

"About time, I'm starving." He claps his hand on my shoulder. "Let's eat."

While we eat, Kate tells me all about their adventures in Italy. The lasagna is perfection, like a tiny slice of paradise. Kate and Arthur's united culinary skills are unmatched by any other couple I know. When she brings out the tiramisu, I'm practically swooning. This woman knows the way to a man's heart.

"Do you know what tiramisu means in Italian?" Kate's eyes glow with amusement as I take the first bite.

A moan rips from my lips at the decadent bliss on my fork. I shake my head and savor another bite.

"*It makes me happy.*" She chuckles. "That's what the waiter told me. How fitting is that?"

Arthur laughs at her giddy response.

"Makes total sense to me," I say between bites. "I guess *orgasm in a bowl* was taken?"

Kate snorts with laughter. Arthur shakes his head, but I see the smile on his lips.

"Any problems while we were gone?" Arthur changes the subject when Kate takes the plates into the kitchen.

Saturday night with Marcy covered in blood and bruises flashes through my mind. Damn, I guess there's no avoiding it. He'll figure it out the moment he sees her. Better I tell him now and give him time to assimilate the news before he sees Marcy.

"There was an incident." I hold my friend's gaze. "With Marcy."

The muscle in Arthur's jaw ticks. His eyes darken, and his hands clench into fists. "What about Marcy?"

"She went out on a date Saturday. He roughed her up good." I hold up a hand when Arthur looks ready to explode. "She called me when she got home, and I took care of it. A couple of bruises and a nasty cut on the cheek. She was shaken up. So I stayed with her."

Arthur's deceptively calm response leaves me unnerved. "Who did it?"

"She refused to tell me." I'm honest with him, but it's killing me not telling him the whole truth of what happened that night. Between her and me. "Even though she wouldn't come to the ER, I wrote up a report at the hospital in case she decides to file charges."

"But she won't tell you who it was?"

I shake my head. "I didn't push either. She's scared. It brought all that past trauma rushing to the surface. So I stayed at her place on Saturday. It's a good thing I did too, because a cat burglar broke in early Sunday morning and scared the hell out of her."

"What?" Arthur rubs his hand over his face.

"Some young woman with more stealth than sense. I took care of it." I correct myself. "Well, I called Richards and *he* took care of her."

"Richards?" He furrows his brow. "Why didn't you call the cops?"

"Because I didn't need a whole bunch of questions about what happened to Marcy on top of everything else. She didn't need that circus either." I shake my head. "You remember what happened the last time."

"Yeah." Arthur relaxes a bit, his hands flexing against the table's surface. "But she's all right?"

"Marcy? Yeah, she's good. Tougher than she looks." I sip my wine.

"I'll check on her tomorrow." My friend slumps back in his chair looking exhausted. "Fuck. Why didn't she tell me when I called her last night?"

"She probably didn't want you to worry. You can get a little overbearing when you're all worked up." I smile. "It's not a bad thing, but sometimes she wants to fight her own battles, big brother. You can't do it for her."

"I know…but shit, I hate feeling so damned helpless."

"Amen to that." I salute him with the glass.

"Thanks for coming to her rescue."

"It's the least I could do."

My stomach twists in knots. I should tell him that we hooked up. But I don't think he needs to hear how many times I railed his little sister after confessing my longstanding affection for her the same night as two traumatic events.

"I should go. It's been a long day."

Kate appears with a frown. "Leaving so soon?"

"Yeah, it's been a long week."

She laughs. "It's only Wednesday."

"It's Friday in my mind thanks to these eighteen-hour shifts." I kiss her on the cheek. "Thanks for dinner. It hit the spot."

Arthur shakes my hand. "Thanks again for everything. The Black Penny on Friday night?"

"Sounds great." I head for the door, petting Tabby on my way out.

The emptiness of my apartment leaves a lot to be desired, but I'm too tired to care. With a full belly, the exhaustion sinks in fast. I manage to change into sleep pants before collapsing into bed. My head hits the pillow, and I'm sinking into dreamland fast.

Shit. I forgot to call Marcy. Fuck.

Sleep evades me, and I stare at the ceiling, wondering if she's going to kill me for neglecting her all week. It's not that I wanted to. Far from it.

I want her all the time. Her company. Her conversation. Her pussy clenched around my cock. Her taste on my tongue. I want all of her. But I haven't figured out how to convince her to take the next logical step.

Now that I've had her, I want everything. Nothing will fill this ache in my chest. I should know; I've tried to fill it before. Marcy's the only one I want.

I love her, and I don't want to live without her. But how the hell do I make her see sense?

I'm not like them.

Shit. Time's ticking, and I'm not getting any younger. I'd rather negotiate with a strung-out addict than Marcy. She's dead set on remaining single. But I've tasted what we could have together. So has she. Maybe it's time I upped the ante.

CHAPTER SEVENTEEN
MARCY

I miss him. When I woke alone on Monday morning and my heart ached at his absence, I told myself it wasn't a big deal. The feeling would wear off. But it hasn't. It's gotten worse.

I tried to call him, but no answer. He must be working overtime at the hospital. It's nothing personal. Right? We each have our own lives and careers. I have plenty to keep me busy this week. I refocus my attention away from the multiple orgasms Rob gave me during our time together over the weekend.

Monday and Tuesday were spent reorganizing inventory for the upcoming summer spectacular event hosted by MTV. Today, I spent all day going over the books with my accountant and the upcoming month's schedule. By the time I make it home, it's after nine.

My apartment feels empty without Rob. He filled that space without effort, making it feel more like a home than it has since I moved in. I toss my purse on the couch just as the doorbell rings.

"Who the fuck…" I trudge to the door and peek out the peephole. Of course. I open the door for my brother. "When did you get back?"

"Yesterday, right before I called you to tell you I was home."

Oh yeah, I forgot that.

He stands like a concrete pilar in my doorway. "Are you going to invite me in?"

"With that scowl on your face, no." I sigh at the pathetic twitch of his lips and step aside, sweeping my arm wide in invitation. "Please, come in."

He scans the apartment while I close and lock the door. "Is

anyone here?"

"No. I just got home from work." I push past him and open the refrigerator. "Want a drink?"

"I'm fine."

"Suit yourself." I grab the open bottle of chardonnay and pour a glass. "So what brings you over so late?"

"What the hell happened?" Arthur reaches out and touches my cheek.

"Nothing." I shove his hand away. He's always too protective, too observant, but I don't feel like rehashing it right now.

"Bullshit, Marcy." He puts his hands in his pockets, and his eyes narrow. "Rob came over for dinner."

"Fuck." I down my wine in one swallow.

"Anything you want to tell me?" His patience burrows a hole in my conscience.

"No."

"I'm your brother. You can't hide this shit from me." His tone softens. "Rob told me someone roughed you up."

"Rob's got a big mouth."

"He came to your rescue, and he's my friend. Why would you think he'd keep this from me?" Arthur cocks his head, studying me with his all too observant eyes. At my silence, he continues. "He told me he was here during the break-in too."

"Oh great." I twist the glass in my hand.

"Marcy, if you don't feel safe here, you're welcome to stay with me and Kate." He clears his throat when overwhelming emotion seeps into the words. "You're family, and I want you safe."

"Thanks, but I'll pass." I fidget in my seat. "It's too close to…"

Rob. I can't bring myself to say it. It sounds stupid. I don't want to sound weak and helpless. And I certainly don't want Rob to think I'm desperate. Even if I do miss him, I can't be that close. No matter how much I want him in my life and my bed.

"Too close to what?" Arthur presses.

"Nothing. Never mind."

"No, it's not nothing." He sits on the couch beside me and takes my hand. "Whatever's going on, you don't have to face it alone. Kate and I love you too much to see you struggle in silence. Rob's worried about you too."

"Of course he is." I meet my brother's gaze.

"I don't know why you hate him so much. He's practically part of the family."

The words strike my heart with a force that leaves me breathless. *He's more than that,* I want to scream. He's everything I've ever wanted, ever dreamed of.

But I'm too damaged, too broken. There aren't fairy-tale endings and rainbows waiting for me. I'm a magnet for assholes who treat me like shit.

Rob's different. He's too pure, too righteous. He deserves a woman who isn't shattered and terrified of commitment.

"I know," I whisper as tears well up in my eyes.

"Look, he didn't tell me all the details. He just wanted to check on you, make sure you're okay."

"Why didn't he do it himself then?"

"He's been working all week. Double shifts." He pats my hand. "I'm sure he'll check on you this weekend, once he has a break."

"Sure." I nod, ignoring the twisting guilt in the pit of my stomach.

Does Arthur know something happened between us? I mean, he's not blind, but I'm not volunteering any information. Not tonight. My body twitches and I stand, unable to sit under his scrutiny.

"You don't look convinced." His gaze follows me. "Did something else happen?"

"No." I bite the edge of my fingernail. "Isn't it bad enough I got beat up and robbed in the same night?"

"I wasn't talking about that." He cocks his head and furrows his brow. "Rob…did you two have a fight or something?"

Images of Rob with his head buried between my thighs flash to the forefront of my mind. My body tingles at the reminder of his warm mouth and talented fingers. I shake my head, trying to purge the wicked, tempting thoughts from my brain.

"No. Nothing like that." My tone is too adamant, and I take a deep breath.

"Something happened between you two. I've been friends with Rob long enough to know when he's not being completely honest." He rises slowly to his feet. "And you…well, I know when you're keeping things from me."

"Nothing happened between Rob and me." I hold his gaze determined to make him believe me. Willing him to believe my blatant lie. "He came over, patched me up, saved me from the cat burglar, and that's it. End of story."

"Okay. Fine. It just seems like you're both a bit on edge now." He lifts his hands in supplication.

"After everything that happened, you expect me not to be?" I scoff.

"That's not what I meant, and you know it."

"Then what are you trying to say?"

"Look, I know you and Rob aren't exactly friends. I'm not even sure when the animosity started between you two." He rakes his fingers through his hair. "But Rob's not your enemy."

"I know that."

"Then stop treating him like he is." Arthur exhales sharply. "He's trying to be nice, the least you could do is to not act like you want to claw his eyes out every time he walks into the room."

"He walked away completely unscathed this weekend."

"Did he?" He arches a brow, frown firmly in place.

Guilt burrows deep into my bones. *Did he really?* I shake my head to clear the invasive thought.

"Listen, I'm not going to pry into your personal life. You've done a hell of a job getting yourself back on track after Dan. I'm proud of you and all you've accomplished." He sighs. "I just don't want to see you throw it all away over another asshole."

Even if he's not an asshole and your best friend? I swallow the retort, knowing I won't like the conversation that follows.

Rob isn't asking me to throw away my career or my dreams. It was one night. I have no idea where it's going to go from here. That's the part that scares the hell out of me.

"Thanks," I mumble, my head spinning with the hundred possible directions this conversation could go if I pursue it. Instead, I wrap my arms around my brother's waist and lay my cheek against his chest.

He squeezes me against him and kisses my forehead. "I love you, Marcy. I just want you to be happy."

"I love you too."

Arthur releases me. "I'll let you get some sleep. Call me if you need anything."

"Will do. Tell Kate I said 'hi.'" I walk him to the door and lock it behind him before collapsing against it and closing my eyes.

Why didn't I just tell him the truth? Because it's Arthur, and he's known Rob for years. I don't want to start some ridiculous feud between them because we hooked up. My brother is protective of me, but he respects my decisions.

After a soothing shower to cool off, I pull on my pajamas and curl up in bed.

I washed the sheets, but the pillow still smells like him. The memories, like whisps of smoke, curl around me, pulling me into a play-by-play review of every sexual act we indulged in.

Rob has always been my dream, my fantasy. Crushing on him as a teen was hard because I knew he would never see me as more than Arthur's little sister. Then after Dan…well, I was broken and scared. I didn't want or need a man to rescue me. But Rob stood beside me, as steadfast as any brother. Never asking for anything, never pushing me.

How I convinced myself he hated me, I'll never understand. Rob's always been there. My knight in bloody scrubs. I pushed him away because this feeling, it terrifies me.

I love Rob, and I always have.

But what the hell am I supposed to do now that we've crossed that line?

Maybe it's time we sit down and have an adult conversation. I need to know what he expects from me.

But first, I need to figure out what I want from him. Am I really willing to break my own vow? Being Rob's wife doesn't sound bad now that I've had time to think about it. I mean, time to seriously consider it.

Sleep evades me while my brain struggles to make sense of my change in plans. I hug Rob's pillow to my chest and inhale deeply, wishing he were here with me now.

Chapter Eighteen
Rob

"Sir, you can't just barge in here like that." Summer's voice carries through the waiting room.

"I must speak with him now."

Wait…I know that voice. Following the sound of commotion, I open the door to the waiting room and see my best friend arguing with one of the nurses.

"It's all right, Summer. I'll handle it." I chuckle when she shakes her head and turns away in a huff.

Arthur faces me. "Finally. I tried to catch you before you left this morning."

"My shift started at four a.m." I hold the door for him. "Come on. My office is back here."

The handful of patients waiting to be seen follow us with curious stares. I don't have much time, but Arthur looks agitated and I don't need an incident in the waiting room. There are far too many of those every day or so as it is.

Summer glances at us as we pass her. "The patient in five is ready for you."

"I'll be there in a moment." I push open my office door and motion for my friend to enter. "Thank you, Summer." With a wink in her direction, I close the door.

"Now, what's so important—"

My words die when Arthur turns around, grabs the lapel of my lab coat, and shoves me against the wall.

"What happened between you and Marcy this weekend?"

"I told you what happened." I grab his fist and slowly peel it from my coat.

"Bullshit." He releases me with a growl and takes a step back. "Something changed between you two. Did you sleep with my sister?"

Shit. This is not how I wanted him to find out, nor is it the best place to discuss it.

"Did Marcy tell you?" My hand runs along my jaw.

"No. She didn't. And neither did you." Arthur's eyes darken. "I figured it out on my own since you're both too chicken shit to admit it like grown adults."

"When did you figure it out?"

"Last night. When I went over to my sister's place. I wanted to check on her after what you said at dinner." He sinks into the chair against the wall. "I offered her a place to stay until she felt safe to be on her own, but she turned me down."

"Sounds like Marcy." I sit in the chair opposite him.

"She's so damned stubborn." He shakes his head. "I just wanted to make sure she was safe."

"Is she?"

"I guess. Hell, I don't know anymore. When I asked her what happened, she gave me the same story you did."

"What tipped our hand?"

"She didn't curse your name when I asked if you two got into a fight." He scoffs. "You two are always at odds with each other. Normally, she gets a sour look on her face when your name comes up, but this time...she smiled."

Relief fills me. "You say that like it's a bad thing."

"It's not. It's just different."

"Change can be a good thing, Arthur."

He nods. "You're right. But this year has been *all* change. It's a bit overwhelming...in a good way." His gaze holds mine. "I just want to be sure Marcy's taken care of. She's strong, but she's also fragile. I don't want her to go through that hell again."

"You really think I'd let that happen?" I rest my hand on Arthur's shoulder. "I've loved Marcy for years. Years, damn it. I will never let anyone hurt her again. Not while she's with me. Not while there's life in my body."

"I know, Rob. That's the only reason I didn't come through the door swinging." He smiles.

"At least you're not pissed off about it."

"Oh, I was. Kate calmed me down before she let me leave

the house this morning."

"What did Kate have to say about it?"

"She told me you two were made for each other. She's seen the sparks fly between you firsthand." He chuckles. "I didn't want to admit it, but she's right. Even when you two were fighting, there were fireworks. I just refused to admit to myself that my best friend and my sister could be happy together."

Hearing those words set my heart free. For years, I worried about what Arthur would say or do if I confessed my affection for his sister, but now I feel as though a weight has been lifted. I'm free to pursue the woman I want without concern about losing my best friend.

"I promise, I will protect her with every fiber of my being." The vow seals over my heart. "I will love her until I draw my dying breath."

"So you want to marry her?"

"Absolutely. If she'll have me."

"That's good. I'm glad to hear it." He strokes his jaw. "Have you told her this?"

"No." Shame floods me. "I was planning on telling her over dinner this weekend, once my last shift ends."

"Better sooner than later." Arthur stands and offers his hand. I shake it. "Good luck."

"Thanks. I know she's not interested in getting married again, but I can hope. Right?"

Arthur laughs, and the booming sound echoes in my small office. "You've known her long enough to know that's going to be a long and bloody battle, my friend. But if anyone can make Marcy see the value in marriage, it's you."

"I love her. I'll wait as long as it takes, do whatever it takes."

He pulls me into a brief hug and shakes his head. "If you need backup, let me know. Kate and I are rooting for you."

"Thanks."

With a final goodbye, Arthur heads down the hall toward the exit. As I watch him walk away, my heart aches. I really need to talk to Marcy. Now more than ever. She has to know how much I love her.

But I've never said the words before. Ever. No woman has ever earned them. Marcy has. She has all my love. I would die for her.

"Dr. Thompson," Summer's voice cuts through my thoughts. "Five is still waiting for you."

"Yes, of course, my apologies." I take the chart she offers and skim through the notes.

It takes every ounce of effort to push thoughts of Marcy to the back of my mind while I work. Summer catches me daydreaming a few times and directs my attention back to the task at hand. I don't know what I'd do without the stellar nursing staff.

After ten years working here, I'm loath to leave them. We've become such a great team and have earned the recognition of the city three years in a row as the best emergency center in Manhattan. I don't know how I would function without them.

But weeks like this one wear on me. I'm exhausted, and now that I have Marcy, there's hope for something more than just emergencies and adrenaline-fueled shifts.

If I can get Marcy to say yes, maybe, just maybe, I can start my own practice and take some time to enjoy life with the woman I love. At least, it's worth considering now.

By four o'clock, I'm dragging. I've pulled eighteen-hour shifts, but ten is still exhausting. Especially after a week of back-to-back double shifts. One hour left, then I can go home and get some rest.

"Oh, my! I didn't even know he was dating anyone." Summer's voice drifts up from the nurse's station. She snaps to attention along with three other nurses when I round the corner.

"Who's dating again?" I ask, wondering if they're gossiping about me and just got caught red-handed.

"Oh, it's, uh…just this actor," Anne, the receptionist, says with a dreamy smile. "He's Hollywood's most eligible bachelor, but I guess he's off the market now." Her smile fades with a sigh.

"We don't have anything better to do than gossip about celebrities?" I chuckle.

"Yes, sir." The nurses return to work, but Summer lingers.

"Did you think we were talking about you?" She jabs me in the side with her elbow.

"Maybe. I don't know. You all seem to like talking about my personal life."

"Oh, you have one of those now?"

I scoff with mock indignance. "I'll have you know, I just found a wonderful woman who doesn't take advantage of my sensitive nature."

"Are you sure you're not just making her up?"

"She's real." I grin. "And she's amazing."

"Hmm, that's why you were glowing when you came in on Monday, huh? Finally got some action, Doc?" Summer laughs as we make our way down the hall to the last room where a patient waits for evaluation.

"I can't help it if you're jealous." I quickly sober when we reach the room.

The young woman looks up from the magazine she's reading. "Sorry." She tosses it onto the chair beside her.

My attention follows the colorful paper, but the moment it settles on the plastic seat, I freeze.

No, that can't be right. I snatch up the magazine and inspect the cover.

Vic Simmons Spied at Romantic Dinner with Mystery Woman is splayed across the front, over a photograph of a couple at an intimate meal.

"Oh shit." My brain replays Marcy's words over and over. Her insistence on not revealing the name of the man who hurt her. "Excuse me for a moment."

Summer covers my lapse as I toss the magazine on the bed and dart from the room.

This can't be happening. No. No. No. I reach the front desk and ask Anne for the magazine she was reading. She hands it to me with a curious look.

Different magazine, similar photograph. Only in this one, I recognize the sweep of her hair, the curve of her jaw, those lips I've tasted. Marcy on a romantic date with Hollywood hotshot, Vic Simmons. Son of a bitch.

He's the bastard who hurt her.

CHAPTER NINETEEN
MARCY

Today's the day. After work, I'm going straight over to Rob's and we're talking this out. It's been horrible trying to focus this week without knowing what's in his head. We need to figure this out. Period.

On the subway to work, I get a few more stares than usual. It must be the fishnet stockings and leather skirt. Maybe the neon top is too much? Doesn't matter. I want Madonna energy today, and I'm damn proud of my effort. Shrugging it off as typical New York, I continue with the commute by diving into the fashion magazine Liana gave me yesterday.

The moment I walk in the door, all hell breaks loose. Liana and Donna rush toward me. Their voices overlap as they ramble, and I can't make sense of the words.

"Whoa, slow down. What happened?"

"You haven't seen?" Donna turns to Liana. "She doesn't know."

"Shit." Liana darts down the hall and returns with a magazine. "You're front-page news."

"What?" I nearly choke on my gum after I take the magazine from her hands. *Vic Simmons Spied at Romantic Dinner with Mystery Woman.* Fear grabs me by the throat and squeezes. There on the cover is a photograph of Vic and me at the restaurant on Saturday night. Fuck. Fuck. Fuck. I pinch my eyes closed, praying it's a joke.

"That's you, right?" Liana points to the woman sitting across from Vic. "I'd recognize you anywhere."

"You went out with Vic Simmons and didn't tell us?" Donna gapes at me.

"Well, yeah, but it was just dinner. Nothing happened. I'm not dating Vic Simmons." My hand covers the cut on my cheek.

"It was nothing."

"Hold on." Liana pulls my hand away and sucks in a breath. "Did he do that?"

"What? No. I fell, hit the corner of a table."

"Uh-huh. That's interesting. Because Monday you told me a cat scratched you, and the bruise was from an errant swinging door." Donna crosses her arms. Her eyes darken like a storm over the bay. "Spill it, sister."

"It's fine. Forget it." I shove Liana's hand away. Panic pulses thick around me, and I need space to breathe. Pushing past them, I head for my office. More tabloids litter my desk. I shove them all into the trash and sit down.

Taking out the checklist for the following week's jobs, I read the words, but nothing sticks. My mind swarms with building anxiety. What if Rob sees this? What if he finds out who I was with on Saturday? He'll know. Fuck.

I bite my lip and try to focus on the list. Tears prick my eyes.

"Honey." Liana's concerned face appears in my doorway. "You don't have to hide it from us. We saw the bruises on Monday."

"And the cut," Donna adds, coming in beside Liana. "Why didn't you tell us the truth?"

I sniff and hide the tears. "What truth? It's nothing. Really."

"Did Vic Simmons do this?" Donna sits on the edge of my desk.

My lip trembles as the memories slam into me with the force of a speeding train colliding with a brick building. Vic's harsh words. His hot breath. The unwelcome pressure of his mouth on mine. His firm grip. The pain shooting through my head when his hand collided with it. The sting of his ring slicing my cheek with the backhand.

I squeeze my eyes closed willing the memories to vanish. But they're replaced by darker, hazier visions of Dan throwing me to the ground. Punching me. Hitting me until I black out in a bloody heap.

"Shh, honey, it's okay," Donna whispers in my ear as she rocks me in her arms.

I'm sobbing. Decimated by memories of the two men who used me and then abused me. Every ounce of strength I've built falls away, and I find myself weak and vulnerable once more. This time, the whole world is watching.

They will recognize me. The photograph is clear as day. There is no way I can tell anyone the truth of that night. No way in hell. They will never believe me over Hollywood's most eligible bachelor.

"Tell us what happened." Liana retrieves the tissues from a small table and offers one. I blow my nose and blink up at them.

As I recount the evening's events, they listen with rapt attention. Both of them flinch when I get to the confrontation in the hallway. Anger replaces their shock when I finish the story.

"Marcy," Donna murmurs. "You can't let him get away with this."

Liana offers another tissue, and I take it with gratitude. I wipe away the tears while shaking my head. "No one will believe me."

"Did you go to the ER?" Liana asks, sitting in the chair across from me.

"No." I hang my head. "I went straight home."

"Did you speak to anyone after that?" Donna presses. "Anyone who can testify to what happened."

Rob's face rises in my mind. His sweet, caring smile. His strong jaw and gentle eyes. "Yeah. I, uh, called a friend. He's a doctor. He came over and took care of my injuries."

"Yes. Good. So he can testify on your behalf." Liana beams.

I shake my head. "No, he can't."

"Why not?" Donna asks.

"Because I refused to tell him who did it." A fresh round of tears springs to my eyes. "If I told him, he'd rush off and try to defend my honor."

"And that's a bad thing?"

"Yeah. They'll arrest him for assault. There's no proof. No one saw Vic and me in the hallway. No one saw him hit me." My hands tremble as I take another tissue. "There's nothing to back my story."

"This was at the Plaza?" Liana taps a finger on her jaw.

"Yeah, why?"

"My cousin Milo works at the front desk there. I could make some calls and see if there's any chatter?"

Hope blooms, then quickly shrivels to dust. "What will it matter? No one will go against Vic Simmons. He'll deny the whole thing."

Donna hugs me tight. "It's okay. We'll figure this out."

"It's hopeless. And now Rob'll discover the truth, and he'll—"

"Rob?" Liana cocks her head.

"The doctor who helped me. He's my brother's best friend and my…" I can't even bring myself to say the words. *Friend. Lover. My heart and soul.*

A knowing look passes between Liana and Donna.

"You love him, don't you?" Donna rubs my back. I know she's not talking about Vic. Her words strike straight to the center of the problem.

"Yeah. I do."

Both of them burst into radiant smiles.

"Finally." Liana sighs. "We've been hoping you'd find a good man."

"But what will I do? He'll find out sooner or later, and then it'll be a shitstorm." I bury my face in my hands.

"Well, first things first. We need to make some calls and find out if someone saw you two in the hallway at the hotel on Saturday night." Liana stands and reaches for the door. "While I do that, Donna will call her lawyer friend and have him come over right away. We need to get these vultures under control before they make a bigger mess."

"What should I do?" I ask, uncertain any of this was going to make a difference. Vic is so influential and popular. How can I go up against that kind of power?

"Go splash some water on your face. Fix your makeup and be ready." Donna grins. "We're going to war."

"You realize this could amount to nothing, right?" I slowly stand, the weight of it all pressing on my shoulders. "This is Vic

Simmons you're talking about."

"Listen. My ex was charming and sweet to everyone, but when it was just us, he was an asshole with a bad temper." Liana's eyes sharpen at the recollection. "I wasn't the first woman he beat, and I'm sure I'm not the last. If Vic hit you, there've been others. We just need to find them."

Donna nods. "Maybe if you speak up, it'll be enough to inspire other women to do it too."

"We can't let him get away with this so he can hurt the next girl." Liana holds my gaze and nods with confidence. "It only takes one with courage to bring the others forward. Are you willing to do that?"

Her words infuse me with determination. "Yes. Let's do this."

"Good." Liana disappears down the hall.

When I head for the door, Donna stops me. "We'll make sure this bastard pays for what he did."

"Thanks." I swallow the emotion lodged in my throat. The moment I reach the bathroom down the hall, I collapse against the sink. My chest tightens, my breathing shallow and panicked.

Facing myself in the mirror, I focus on deep breaths until the wave passes. My makeup is smeared, and I look like a wilting Salvador Dali painting. I grab a washcloth and soap and scrub my face.

The purpling bruises and small gash healing on my cheek are highlighted by the lack of product. Rather than reapply my makeup, I smear on some lotion and wear the injuries with pride. When the lawyer shows up, I want him to see what Vic did to me without the mask of makeup protecting my wounded ego.

I should call Rob, tell him before he sees it on the news. It's not something I want to tell him over the phone, but he's at work. I have until he gets off at five to get this shitstorm under control and catch him at home.

I'd rather him hear it from me than the tabloids, but it may be too late.

CHAPTER TWENTY
ROB

Fucking finally. At five o'clock, I gather my stuff and bolt out of the ER.

It took every ounce of strength I possess not to storm out of the hospital and make a beeline for Marcy's office the moment I saw that magazine. Summer tried to ask me about it, but I didn't have the time or patience to explain it. Not when I needed to get across town and see her.

I hail a cab and give the driver her address. The entire trip is spent in torment, wondering what in the hell I am going to say, what she will do when I confront her.

She wouldn't tell me who hurt her, wouldn't go to the ER. But the truth is she couldn't. Vic Simmons is a Hollywood superstar. He has leagues of lawyers and agents who would throw themselves into the flames to protect their client. Especially a moneymaker like Vic. Even if Marcy came forward and filed an incident report with the police, they would sweep it under the rug. No one would be the wiser.

It's a damned disaster. I have half a mind to hunt the bastard down and make him pay for what he did to her. But where would that land me? Prison, that's where. And pretty boy would get off scot-free.

Fury bubbles up inside me. By the time I reach her apartment, it's a full-on inferno. I pay the cabbie and step back from the curb. A flash of neon catches my eye.

Marcy. She's walking toward the door to her building, her arms wrapped around her torso. It's mid-May and nearly ninety degrees, but she looks like she's shivering in the cold.

"Marcy!" I call out with a wave.

She comes to a stop, her gaze snaps up at the sound of her name. Then she spots me through the crowd of pedestrians filling the sidewalk. As I make my way closer to her, her eyes widen. At this distance I can't tell if it's out of fear or relief, but it doesn't matter.

"Rob, what are you doing here?"

I pull her against me. Her arms wrap around my waist, and her tense body relaxes. "I came to check on you."

When I draw back, I tip her chin up and search those mesmerizing eyes. Gone is the heavy eye shadow and dark liner. Without makeup, the bruises stand out against her pale skin. The cut is healing nicely, but it's still an angry red blemish against her porcelain skin.

Fury rises hot and heavy inside me at the sight. "I can't believe that bastard hit you."

"Not here," Marcy hisses. "Come on, let's go inside."

Without waiting for my agreement, she drags me by the hand to her apartment. Silence fills the elevator on the way to her floor.

Once we're safely tucked inside her apartment, I round on her. "You could have told me it was Simmons, Marcy. I would have believed you."

Marcy scoffs and skirts around me, heading for the kitchen. "It doesn't matter. It's over, I can't take it back. And if I could, I would give him a pair of swollen nuts to go with his oversized ego."

"That's not the point. You should have told me. I could have—"

"Could have what? Called the cops? Filed a report? Made me go to the ER?" She shelves her hand on her hips. "I know you, Rob. You would have stormed over to his hotel and punched him in the face."

"I have more restraint than that." I huff. "Give me some credit."

"It's not worth getting the cops involved." She shuffles her feet uncomfortably and grabs orange juice from the refrigerator. "Dan beat me to within an inch of my life."

"Not worth…" I cross the space between us and grip her arms. "Look at me, Marcy." She lifts her gaze, and I see the uncertainty swimming deep within her. "You're worth it. I don't care who he is, but he shouldn't be given a pass because of his celebrity status."

"He won't." Her jaw ticks. "I've already hired a lawyer and started the process."

I blink at her twice. "What?"

"Liana and Donna convinced me to file charges."

When I release her, she pours a glass of orange juice. Her voice wavers. "I spoke to the lawyer. He's going to start the process."

"That's great." Relief fills me, but the joy doesn't quite reach her smile. "Wait, what's the problem?"

"There aren't any witnesses to the actual assault." She sips the juice. "We were in a dark hallway. If there's no witness, there's no case. It'll be my word against his, and his agency will pay to keep me quiet. It'll all get swept under the rug."

"I can serve as a witness to your state after the incident. If I file a report in the hospital system, we can use it in the case."

"I appreciate that, but it won't help." She sighs. "Unless we can find someone who saw what happened in that hotel hallway, it's a lost cause." Her expression falters.

I gather her in my arms, and she rests her head back against my chest. "I'm sorry."

"I haven't given up hope completely." Her voice rumbles through me, and the sweet scent of her shampoo teases my sense of reason. I shove aside the temptation to drag her into the bedroom and make her forget about everything except for the pure explosive pleasure I give her.

"What do you mean?"

She arches back against me, and my hands tighten around her waist. "Liana's cousin works at the Plaza. She called and told him what happened on Saturday. He wasn't working, but he knows who was. He's making some inquiries among the staff to see if anyone happened to see Vic and me in the hallway."

Hope unfurls in my chest. If they're able to find a witness, it changes everything. I kiss her on the back of the head.

"Come on." I nudge her toward the bedroom.

"Where are we going?" She nearly drops the glass, setting it aside in haste.

"Pack a bag. You're staying with me until we figure this shit out."

"Why?" She spins around and glowers at me. "I'm not fucking helpless, Rob. I don't need a babysitter."

"Listen—until this shit blows over, I don't think you should be alone."

Her exasperated look brooks no argument.

I relent. "Fine. If you don't want to stay with me, at least stay with your brother and Kate."

Her nose scrunches at the suggestion. "I don't want to be in the apartment alone with those two honeymooners."

"Then stay with one of your other friends."

"But I want to stay here."

"It's only a matter of time before they figure out who you are and where you live." I rest my hands on her shoulders. "Before you know it, you're going to have paparazzi camped around your home and your office. Trust me. You're in the spotlight, whether you like it or not. The best thing you can do right now is lay low."

"You're right." She frowns, and I want to smooth the lines between her brows with my thumb. "I hate that you're right."

I can't help but smile at the win. "Okay, go pack a bag."

Marcy pauses in the doorway to her bedroom, resting her hand on the frame. "Were you serious?"

"About what?"

"Letting me stay with you?" She draws her lower lip between her teeth, and I suppress a growl of protectiveness.

"Of course." I take two steps and pull her into my arms. "For as long as you want."

My lips nearly spill the word *forever* but it's a delicate time. I don't want to push her. We'll talk about *us* later once we're at my place.

Twenty-five minutes later, I'm wheeling her suitcase to the curb and hailing a cab. Marcy climbs in beside me and gives the cabbie my address. I pull her against me to kiss her temple. She leans her head against me, and we ride in silence.

I like this. Having her nestled by my side, certain of her safety.

"We should tell Arthur." Her voice drifts up on a murmur.

"You should." I hold her tight. "He'll find out sooner or later. It's best if he hears it from you."

"I'm sorry." She sniffs. "I should have told you."

"It's okay. I'm just glad you're safe."

"How did you find out?" She leans back and searches my face.

"Some of the nurses were talking about it, and I saw the photo on a magazine cover."

She winces. "I should have told you."

"It doesn't matter now, baby." I press a soft kiss to her lips. "Let's make sure your brother doesn't find out the same way. I don't think he'll take it as well as I did."

"You took it well?" She scoffs.

"Hell no. I was about to tear the ER apart." Her smile warms my soul. "If I ever see him, I'll rip him to shreds."

"Don't." Marcy shakes her head, eyes wide. "Don't make it more complicated than it already is."

Something about her tone soothes the furious beast inside me. I nod and pull her into my arms once more. I love this woman. It feels so good to finally hold her.

And I'm never letting go. Until death do we part.

CHAPTER TWENTY-ONE
MARCY

Arthur is going to lose his shit.

Rob squeezes my hand and knocks on the door of my brother's penthouse. "It'll be fine," he whispers in my ear when the lock rattles against the door.

Inhaling a deep breath as it opens, I brace myself for the oncoming storm. Kate's kind smile greets us.

"I was just about to call you!" Kate steps aside, inviting us in. Her voice drops low. "I saw the headlines. What's going on?"

"Is Arthur home?" Rob glances around the empty apartment.

"He just got here." She nods toward the bedroom. "He's changing."

Nervous energy skitters along my spine. Rob's grip tightens on my hand. His hazel eyes meet mine, reminding me that I'm not alone. He's right beside me.

"I'll let him know you're here. Help yourself to a drink." Kate takes two steps before Rob's question stops her.

"Does he know?"

Kate shakes her head. "I'm glad you're here. He'll take it better if it comes from you, Marcy."

I nod, unable to trust my voice. Rob leaves me in the living room, retreating to the side bar to pour two whiskeys. When he returns, he places one in my hand with a confident smile.

"This'll take the edge off."

"Thanks." I down it, letting the drink warm me through.

Déjà vu. A piss-poor decision has led me to my brother's doorstep once again. I want to melt into the carpet. *But it's different this time.* Yeah, it is. This time I was smart enough to know when to walk away. This time I have Rob beside me, giving me courage to do what I need to do.

His solid presence infuses me with courage. How was I so stupid for so long? Thinking he disliked me. Thinking him indifferent to my presence.

The signs had been there all along, and I was too fucking blind to see them. Rob didn't save me; he supported me. He cared when he could have walked away.

"Marcy." Arthur joins us. "Rob. To what do I owe the pleasure?" His gaze fixes on my face.

"I made a mistake." I swallow the lump in my throat. "Kate, do you have the magazine?"

"Yeah." She edges around Arthur and retrieves it from the kitchen. When she hands it to me, I clutch it to my chest, like a shield blocking my heart.

"What happened?" Arthur's scowl deepens.

"I wanted to tell you, show you, before you read about it in the tabloids." With a deep breath, I press on. "One of my clients invited me to dinner last Saturday. I said yes, and we were photographed together."

Rob takes the magazine from my hand and gives it to Arthur. The furrow between his brows deepens even further, and the kind face of my older brother skews into horror and disbelief.

"Is this the man who hurt you?" His gravelly voice is menacing.

If I had been worried about Rob's reaction, I was terrified of my brother's. Both men were overly protective of me, but since my divorce, Arthur has made it his life's mission to keep me from experiencing that pain again.

"Yes." I hold his gaze steady as I elaborate on the events of that night and the startling revelation of our relationship in the tabloids.

"I see." He clenches the magazine in his fist. "Have you filed charges?"

"My lawyer is working on it." The pressure of Rob's hand on mine encourages me. "But unless there's a witness, it's hopeless. His status will give him indemnity. Between his agents and the press, any whisper of wrongdoing will be swept under the rug, and there's nothing I can do about it."

"No one saw you together?" Arthur crosses his arms.

"Oh, people saw us together. Hell, the whole city now knows we were together that night." Bile bites the back of my throat at the thought. "But there was no one around when he hit me. He made sure of it."

"You think he's done this before?" Rob asks with surprise.

"Judging from his reaction, yeah, I think he has a nasty habit of beating women who don't fall at his feet and do what he wants."

"Do you have any proof that this isn't the first time he's done it?" Kate interjects.

I shake my head. "I don't have proof of anything. All I know is that a man of his stature, his status, isn't used to being called out for his shitty behavior. He's all charm until you say no."

"Someone must have seen something." Arthur's agitated movements do nothing to calm my nerves.

"They're making inquiries now with the hotel staff," I add, as though it will soothe him.

Before Arthur can respond, Rob stands up. "Why don't we go down to the Black Penny, see if Richards is around? He might be able to help."

A long look passes between Rob and my brother. Finally, Arthur relents. "Fine." He kisses Kate. "You two stay here. We'll be back in a few hours."

"Wait. You can't seriously expect me to stay locked away while we get this figured out?" I stalk toward them and grab my brother's arm. "I'm coming with you."

He turns to face me. "Listen, your face is plastered all over every tabloid and gossip rag in the city. It's only a matter of time before they figure out your name and where you live." Arthur pulls me into a warm hug. "Let us take care of this part. We'll do some digging, ask some questions. Then, when we have the ammunition, we'll let you take him down."

Arthur lets me go and disappointment fills me.

"I can't let you fight this battle for me." Defiance replaces disappointment. "I won't."

"We're not fighting your battle, Marcy." My brother sighs. "We're supporting you. Let us do this. It's going to be hard enough to face down Vic Simmons in court."

"I relish the opportunity." The thought should scare me, but instead it leaves me vibrating with certainty that this is the right course of action.

"Good. Save your strength. You'll need it for the long haul." Arthur presses a kiss to my forehead. "You've fought alone for years. Let us help you with this."

Deep in my heart, I soften at his touch and his words. "Fine."

Rob tilts my chin up. "Don't worry. We'll find something on him. He won't get away with this." He strokes his thumb across my jaw. "Promise."

The press of his warm lips to mine leaves me clutching his shirt. I don't want to let him go. I love him too much.

"Be careful," I murmur against his mouth.

"Always." With a smile, he and Arthur head out into the spring evening in search of something I'm not sure they'll be able to find. It's a wild-goose chase. Vic Simmons has the media by the balls. No one will cross him.

"Fuck." I slump onto the couch and clutch the pillow to my chest.

"You love him, don't you?" Kate appears beside me with a bottle of wine and two glasses.

"That obvious, huh?" I rest my cheek on the pillow.

"Yeah."

She pours a glass for me. I take it with a muttered thanks.

"I'm glad you two finally got together. I might not have been around long, but these last few months of you two hurling jabs at each other is enough to set the curtains on fire."

"I can't believe I was that blind."

"We all have those moments." Kate chuckles. "But it doesn't matter now. You're both on the same page."

"Are we?" I cradle the glass in my hands. "I mean, this is all so new. We haven't discussed anything yet. All we've done is fuck. Which, don't get me wrong, is nice. Better than nice. It's fantastic. But I don't know what he wants for the future. For us."

"You'll have to ask him." Kate salutes me. "Before you jump him again."

My face heats. "We've both been alone for so long. What if it doesn't work?"

"I guess you won't know until you try." She rests her hand on my knee. "I wouldn't worry about it though. Rob's a cinnamon roll. He'll do anything for you."

"Cinnamon roll?" I skew my nose up at her strange reference. "What do pastries have to do with anything?"

"Shit." Kate laughs, nearly spilling her wine. "Sorry. I keep forgetting. A cinnamon roll is someone who is sweet and kind but faces more hardship and suffering than they deserve."

"That sounds exactly like Rob." I smother a laugh behind my hand.

"I wouldn't worry about Rob. He loves you, and whatever comes next, he'll be right there beside you the whole time."

Emotion chokes me, and all I can do is nod.

"Why don't you help me in the kitchen? I was about to whip up some pork stir-fry with noodles." Kate stands and offers her hand.

My stomach growls at the mention of food. "That sounds amazing."

"Good. I've got everything ready." Kate ventures into the kitchen, but I pause halfway across the room and cast a longing look over my shoulder at the door.

At this point, I don't care about Vic Simmons. I care about Rob. Sweet, caring, wonderful Rob. He's chasing my demons, and I feel like there's nothing I can do to help him.

When he comes back, we'll talk. I don't want to be without him. Not for another moment. Life's too short to waste one more minute apart.

CHAPTER TWENTY-TWO
ROB

"What the fuck are you thinking?" I round on my best friend.

Arthur glares at me as he settles back in the cab. The cabbie pulls away from the curb, heading toward the Plaza Hotel.

"I'm getting answers." He levels me with his gaze.

"We agreed to talk to Richards before heading to the hotel." Uncertainty twists in my gut. "We can't go in there half-cocked."

"Look." Arthur heaves a sigh. "We need to get answers before this spirals out of control."

"Exactly. And that's why we were going to consult Richards before starting an inquisition." I run my hand across my jaw, agitated at the recklessness of his plan. "Maybe we should call Richards and have him meet us there."

"No." He shakes his head. "Once we get there, we'll split up. You take the restaurant. I'll talk to management." His eyes glisten in the decaying sunlight. "Someone *had* to have seen something, damn it."

"Marcy said one of her stylists has a cousin who works at the front desk. Maybe if you drop her name, they'll be more willing to help."

"Which stylist?"

"Liana."

Arthur nods. "Yes, I remember her."

The silence stretches for a few blocks. The knot in my stomach expands the closer we get to the hotel. This could end badly if we don't play it right.

"So what's our story?" I ask as the city descends into darkness around us.

"The truth, but we keep it vague." He meets my gaze, unflinching in his determination. "My sister was here with a date on Saturday. They got into an argument in the hallway outside the restaurant. Did anyone see anything?"

"But what's our reason for asking?"

"Why do we need one?"

I shrug. "We don't, but they're not going to be as willing to talk if we don't have a legitimate reason."

"Then we tell them the truth. He got physical, and she's pressing charges." He cocks his head. "But I wouldn't volunteer that information up front. Let's see how far we can get on charm alone."

The cab pulls up in front of the hotel, and my hands are shaking when I step onto the sidewalk. Arthur pays the cabbie, and together we head into the towering hotel. It's been an intricate fixture in the skyline for years. But tonight isn't for admiring the architecture; it's for getting answers.

There are a few patrons milling around in the lobby. I follow Arthur to the front desk, where he asks for the manager. What did Marcy say Liana's cousin's name was? Miles? Mike? I catch a glimpse of the name tag of the man behind the counter. *Milo.*

"Are you Liana's cousin?" I ask, keeping my voice low.

"Yes." His eyes widen, and his voice drops to a whisper. "Are you here about what happened to Marcy?"

Arthur and I share a look. He nods at the man behind the counter. "Did anyone see anything?"

He nervously licks his lips and glances around, ensuring he can't be overheard. "I didn't. But I asked some of the staff who were working in the restaurant that night. A few of them said they heard arguing in the hallway when they were coming back from their break."

"Can we speak with them?" Hope blooms in my chest, but I tamp it down. Just because they heard arguing doesn't mean they saw anything.

Milo nods and calls over another employee to take his place behind the counter. "Follow me." He leads us to the elevator and up to the restaurant on the fifteenth floor. We pause in the hallway outside the restaurant, near the restrooms. "Wait here."

Arthur and I wait, impatient but quiet, our nerves lit like live wires. Neither of us speaks, but when Milo reappears, I let Arthur take the lead. Milo quickly appraises the waiter of the reason for his presence.

The waiter's eyes shift to us with skepticism. "You sure they're not reporters?" he asks Milo.

"They're not. They're friends of my cousin." Milo turns to us. "Ask him. I'll be at the front desk if you need anything else." He bolts to the elevator, leaving us with the tall waiter.

In this lighting, it's difficult to gauge his age, but I'd say he's not much older than Arthur and me. I offer my hand, and he shakes it. "Sorry to bother you, but we have a few questions about Saturday night."

"So you're cops?" He stiffens.

"No." Arthur steps in. "But my sister was here on Saturday night. About this tall, dark hair, hazel eyes…"

"The girl with Vic Simmons?" He rubs his jaw. "Yeah, I remember those two. Making eyes at each other all night."

My hands clench into fists, but I manage to maintain my composure. "That's her. Did you see them outside the restaurant?"

"I did. They were right there." He points to a dark nook in the bend of the hallway. "I was coming back from a smoke break when I heard arguing. Sounded like someone struggling. I crept close to get a better look, and I saw them making out."

I flinch at his words.

Arthur commandeers the questioning. "Did you see anything else?"

"Yeah, I saw the bastard take a swing at her. He got in two hits before I could react to what I was seeing." He shook his head. "By the time I stepped into view, he'd pulled away. I ducked out of sight again before he could unleash on me. When I came back a moment later, she was gone."

"Why didn't you come forward with this information?" I push, knowing I'm already running with a short fuse.

"To who? There were no cops, no inquiry." He scoffs. "Who's gonna believe me anyway? I didn't know who the girl was, and I wasn't about to lose my job and credibility by going up against Vic Simmons."

My hope deflates at his words. "So you're not willing to testify to what you saw that night?"

"I never said that." He narrows his eyes. "But there better be a solid case before I take the stand against him."

"You'd testify on her behalf?" Arthur asks, holding the man's gaze.

"If I know the bastard will get what he deserves, then yes, I'll testify."

"Why stick your neck out for a woman you don't know?" The question leaves my lips before I can bite it back. I can't just leave well enough alone. I need to know why he'd do something so selfless.

"My dad…he, uh…" The waiter sniffs and drops his gaze. "He beat my mom. No one spoke up for her, and she died."

The confession hangs in the air between the three of us. I can hear the unspoken shame and trauma this man endured. Even more, I sense the undercurrent of regret and guilt gnawing at his heart for not taking action against his father to save his mother.

"I'm sorry." My apology sounds weak, but it's sincere.

"Yeah…well, that was years ago." He clears his throat. "I figure I can do something this time around."

"We appreciate it." Arthur shakes his hand.

After we take his information, he retreats into the restaurant while Arthur and I head to the ground floor. Neither of us speaks until we're in the cab. I give directions for the driver to take us to the Black Penny.

If we get this information to Richards, he can vet the waiter. We can't do this halfway. It has to be airtight.

Vic Simmons will pay for what he did to Marcy.

After a few shots and a long conversation with Richards, we have our next step. He'll run a background check on both the waiter and Simmons. We can take the information to Marcy's lawyer and let him start the process.

I manage to keep it together until I reach my apartment. Inside, Marcy's curled up in my bed, sleeping. Kate must have given her the spare key. I'm fit to burst with all the information I have, but I don't have the heart to wake her.

Once I strip down, I slide beneath the covers beside her. She curls against me, and I'm reminded of just how lucky I am to have her in my life.

She deserves peace, and I'm determined to see this through to the end.

CHAPTER TWENTY-THREE
MARCY

I snuggle in when his arm drapes across my waist, pulling me close. A contented sigh escapes me.

Rob's lips trail over my shoulder, and I squirm trying to get even closer. "I didn't mean to wake you."

"It's fine." I moan when he nips at my skin. "This is the best way to be woken up."

Artificial light filters through the windows, casting a hazy glow across the dark room. I turn in his arms until we're face to face. His careworn expression leaves my heart pounding. For years, I've dreamed of this, of sharing myself with him. This man has seen me at my worst, and yet he still wants me.

I bite my lip. "How did it go with Richards?" I trail my finger along his jaw.

"Good." Rob drops his gaze. "Listen, I don't want you to get upset, but you deserve to know."

"Upset? Why would I get upset?" I draw back slightly.

"Arthur and I went to the Plaza." He holds up a hand when I open my mouth to protest. "We spoke to someone willing to testify on your behalf. He saw everything."

My fury at their presumptuous action disintegrates into shock. "Wait...what?"

"There was a waiter who saw the whole encounter in the hallway. He's willing to testify against Vic Simmons."

"You're joking?"

"I would never joke about something like this." He takes a deep breath and cups my cheek in his palm. "Richards is going to run background checks on him and Simmons, get us some more information before you meet with your lawyer."

"I'm supposed to meet with him tomorrow afternoon."

"Do you want me to go with you?"

He's in earnest. I can see the unresolved agitation in the way he tenses his body as if he's bracing for rejection. "Let me think about it."

"Okay. There's no rush." He deflates at my response but nods in understanding. "I'm here for you, Marcy. Whatever you need, just say the word."

"I appreciate it." My heart aches at the thought of Rob and Arthur fighting my battle for me, even though they have both assured me they're only helping me. "But this whole mess is my fault. I shouldn't have gone out with him. I should have trusted my gut."

"You can't blame yourself for his actions." He hooks his finger beneath my chin and brings my gaze up. "You did nothing wrong. He's an abusive, entitled asshole."

"I know." Tears sting my eyes. "But you of all people should understand…I don't want to be rescued. I don't want charity. Facing him down is the only way I'll get any closure. I refuse to be scared of my own shadow just because he's a goddamn bully."

"I'm not trying to fight this battle for you, Marcy." His touch leaves me trembling with need. "I'm here for support. You've got yourself through worse scrapes than this, and you've thrived because of it. I couldn't be prouder of you than I am right now. Facing this takes courage. There are a lot of people who break under this pressure."

"Trust me, I've been tempted to just walk away and let him win this round." Heaviness settles around my heart at the thought of Vic hurting another woman when I could have stopped the cycle. "I can't bear the thought of someone else being on the receiving end of his unwanted attention. What if he goes too far and does major damage?"

"You're right. He could easily hurt someone or kill them." Rob closes his eyes and exhales sharply. "I've seen it happen more times than I care to remember. Abuse should never be tolerated."

"No one should be subjugated to that." A shiver racks me, regardless of the spring heat.

Rob draws me closer and kisses my forehead. "I'm proud

of you for standing up."

"Rob?" I cling to him, wrapping my leg around his thigh. "Why are you doing this for me?"

"I love you. I've always loved you." His breath ghosts over my cheek.

Fireworks ignite in my chest at those three little words. I close my eyes.

"I want to cherish you. Protect you. Love you. It's all I've ever wanted to do."

"But why?" I ask, inhaling the scent of him and committing it to memory. "I'm broken and difficult."

"We're all broken, sweetheart." He rests his hand on my hip, drawing small circles with his thumb. "But that doesn't mean you're not worthy of my love."

His words leave me breathless and confused, but I hear truth ringing in their depths. I try to disentangle myself from his embrace, but he grips me tighter.

"Don't push me away." His murmured plea makes me stop. "I'm not asking you to get married and start a family. I'm not even asking you to move in with me. I would never ask you to sacrifice anything for us to work. I'm willing to take it slow if that's what you need."

The tears finally spill free. He swipes them away with the pad of his thumb. For years I kept him at arm's length because I was terrified of letting myself feel anything for him. Because I valued him too much to have him disappear from my life if he didn't feel the same way.

"I love you, Rob." A whimper breaks out when the words leave my mouth.

With crushing tenderness, he presses his lips to mine. Every ounce of tension leaves me at the loving expression. He deepens the kiss, exploring with reverence. He pulls me close, pressing our bodies together, tangling our legs and tongues. I want to get lost in him and never resurface.

Rob, with all his faults, is the only man who has ever seen the true me.

The friction building between us reaches the point of

desperation. My hips grind against his thigh. Naked and needy, I climb on top of him, straddling his thighs. He's hard and ready, his cock brushing my slick pussy.

He grips my hips tight as I guide him to where I want him. One thrust and I gasp when he's buried deep inside me. Emotions pulse through me in waves, I rest my head against his chest and take several deep breaths, trying to ground myself.

His hand comes around the back of my neck, tender, soothing against my skin. I meet his gaze. He's grinning. My heart does a little flip.

I buck my hips against his, and a groan of pleasure tears from his throat.

"Do it again, baby." He sucks in a breath when I repeat the action. "Take what you need."

"Oh, I intend to."

Bracing my hands on the bed beside his head, I find my rhythm. His eyes drift closed as I ride his cock, grinding my hips against his to fan the flames higher.

Our mixed moans echo in the dark room. The speed of my panting gasps increases as my orgasm builds. I need more of him, and my release hovers just out of reach.

As if sensing my frustration, Rob switches our positions and drives deeper, pushing me into the mattress. I wrap my legs around him and meet his thrusts with my own.

This is what I want. What I need.

I dig my nails into his skin, holding tight. He kisses me hard, doubling his efforts.

A cry rips from my throat as I reach the pinnacle and tumble over the other side. Pleasure rocks through me with the force of a tidal wave, leaving me trembling and sensitive.

Rob takes his own release. His warmth fills me, leaving me sticky and sated. I've never been more content.

"You okay?" He lifts his weight off me and searches my face.

"I'm fabulous." I arch up and kiss his lips softly.

"Wait here." Rob climbs off the bed and disappears into the bathroom.

"I couldn't move if I tried." I languish in the bed, unable to move my limbs after such an earthshattering climax.

He chuckles from the other room. When he returns, he cleans me with a warm rag and rejoins me. Tucking me against him, he sighs in contentment.

"Why don't we stay home tomorrow?" I muse, half asleep and sex-drunk. "We can stay in bed all day and fuck each other senseless."

"That sounds like a great idea." He groans. "But I have to work."

"What time?"

"Three."

"We have all morning then." I snuggle closer.

"We have our whole lives." He quickly adds, "If that's what you want. No pressure."

My response lodges in my throat.

It is what I want, but I've been alone for so long, I can't jump into something so quickly. Can I?

With Rob by my side, I can do anything. The soft, steady breaths against my shoulder tell me I don't have to answer him tonight. He's fast asleep.

I stare at the wall, wondering what happens next. Is this too good to last?

CHAPTER TWENTY-FOUR
ROB

We spend half the day in bed, wrapped in each other and sheltered from the realities of the world outside. It's heaven, and I never want to leave.

Until I get a call from Arthur at noon. Richards has the reports on Vic Simmons and our witness from the restaurant. He wants to meet and discuss them at the Black Penny.

My call into work leaves my superiors shorthanded, but after all the hours I pulled this week, they can find someone to fill in for me this time. If things go well, I won't be working there much longer anyway. Now that I have Marcy, I have bigger plans that don't include working doubles in the ER.

I press a kiss to Marcy's forehead, and she pulls me in for one last drugging kiss before I leave. She's not thrilled about being left behind, but Kate offered to go with her to the meeting with the lawyer. We'll meet up with them there.

Downstairs, Arthur's waiting for me by a shiny black town car. Cyril gives me a wave from the driver's side. Must be nice to have one's own personal driver in this city. No subway. No taxis. No walking. Just…onward, Cyril.

I slide into the back beside Arthur. "What's the game plan?"

"Richards has the information. We'll meet him first, then head over to Marcy's lawyer."

"What time?"

"Five." He glances at his watch. "I've already given the lawyer an update with the new information. He agrees she should lay low for a while, but she needs to file a formal complaint today to get the charges started. With this, we'll have enough ammunition to get this guy more than a slap on the wrist."

"He deserves a *lot* more than that," I grumble, leaning back against the seat. "I don't think this is the first time he's done it."

"You're probably right." Arthur watches the city pass outside the window.

For the rest of the drive, we're silent. My mind churns over the information, again and again. Personally, I'd like nothing more than to make this asshole disappear forever, but that goes against every ethos I have. This needs to be methodical and focused. I don't want him or the paparazzi coming after Marcy. I just want it over.

When we reach the Black Penny, Claude waves us toward the back where Richards is waiting for us. I slide into the booth across from him, and Arthur takes the space beside me.

"I did some digging, and it took some sweet-talking to get the tyrant in records to release this shit." Richards's eyes flicker with amusement. "Looks like your boy here has a long history of taking things that don't belong to him. Three rape charges, two assaults, and one breaking and entering."

"Holy shit." I run my hand across my jaw as I skim through the reports. My instincts on this asshole were spot-on. "Has he ever been convicted?"

"No." Richards leans back. "Every single case got settled out of court and conveniently swept under the rug."

"Fucking figures." Arthur sneers.

"Do you think these are the only incidents?" I ask Richards.

He shakes his head. "These are only the ones where he got caught. In my experience, there are always more. He's got a taste for it. Gives him a rush. Chances are, there are a lot more, but because of his status, they disappear fast...*if* they come forward at all."

"Is it worth pursuing this?" Arthur asks the question burning in the back of my mind.

"It'll be complicated and drawn out. Because he's a celebrity, it will get national coverage and could get messy. They'll likely try to settle out of court." Richards shrugs.

"But he'll do it again." Anger bubbles within me.

"Yup." Richards takes a drink. "Another thing. If Marcy testifies against him, they'll dig up her past and throw it in her face. You think she's ready for that?"

Arthur and I exchange a long, knowing look. This could get ugly. Really ugly. We've spent years trying to protect Marcy, but this will rip open the scars to bleed anew. Is she willing to put herself through that?

"She can handle it," Arthur replies. "But it'll be hard."

Richards nods. "Okay. I'll make a few calls, see what I can dig up." He takes the folders and tucks them out of sight. "I'll have these delivered to the lawyer when she files the official charges."

"Thanks." I shake his hand, and we part ways.

Cyril has the car waiting for us outside the bar. Arthur gives him an address, and we climb in.

It's a quick ride, barely enough time to compose myself to face the fight I know is coming. It'll be hard to convince anyone to take this fucker on in court. I can only hope her lawyer isn't a chickenshit who'd rather take a plea deal than make the bastard see the inside of a courtroom. If I have to scour the city for someone willing to take this case, then so be it. Marcy deserves a chance at justice. Every one of those women does.

Walking into the building, Arthur falls into step beside me. We take the elevator up, tense silence pulsing around us. I step out onto the twelfth floor and freeze.

Two men are standing outside the office, shaking hands with a third man. The taller one turns, and recognition slams into me with the force of a well-placed punch to the gut.

Vic Simmons. The same smug face I've seen on the cover of countless magazines and movie posters.

He hurt Marcy. *Bastard.*

His gaze fixes on me.

The sound of a door opening behind me makes me turn. Marcy steps into the hall, her eyes bloodshot, her chin raised high. Our eyes meet for a brief moment, but the second she sees Vic beyond us in the hallway, she pivots on her heel and retreats to the exit. Kate follows her, casting an apologetic, concerned glance at Arthur over her shoulder.

He fucking *hurt* her again. I don't even care what he said or did, I saw the look of pain on her face. My control snaps.

"What the fuck did you do to her?"

His eyes widen as I approach, and he lifts his hands in defense. The moment I'm within reach, I strike. Hauling back, I let my fist fly. A perfect jab catches him square in the face. The crunch of his nose breaking mixes with the crack of my knuckles fracturing from the impact. Blood pours from his nose, but he hauls back, throwing a hook, and catches the side of my face.

He lunges for me, and it's World War III. I feel like Rocky but without experience or confidence. The only thing I know is I want this asshole to bleed for what he did. We get a few more hits in before they drag us apart.

Arthur puts himself between Vic and me and hands me a handkerchief. His stern expression fixes on me like I'm a kid caught fighting at school.

"What the hell is your problem?" Vic shouts while two men in suits hold him back.

"That's for what you did to Marcy, asshole." I flip him the bird. "I'll see you in court."

He smirks. Blood stains his teeth. "I doubt that."

I lunge forward again, but Arthur catches me by the arm. "Save it," he growls against my ear. "This isn't the time or the place. Come on." He drags me into the office, out of the hallway.

As Simmons passes, I catch the twisted grin on his lips. He thinks he's won, thinks he's on top of this. But he doesn't know how determined I can be. Fucking with Marcy has earned him a one-way ticket to prison.

"What the hell were you thinking?" Arthur shakes me. "He could come at you with assault charges now."

"He won't." I dab the blood from my face, wincing at the sting and the pulsing throb in my right hand.

"You don't know that." Arthur keeps his voice low as the lawyer approaches.

"Putting himself in the spotlight will only draw more attention to his imperfections." I snort. "Guys like him are self-centered with egos the size of Mount Rushmore. I'd like to see him fucking press charges, then I'll drag his name through the mud."

Arthur shakes his head when the lawyer appears. "Let me do the talking."

"Fine."

I manage to keep calm during the meeting. As I judged from the look on Marcy's face, Vic's team has already intervened and tried to sweep this "misunderstanding" under the rug. The lawyer doesn't seem optimistic about the case should it come to court, unless there are other women who come forward with similar stories. If that were to become the case, then he would be more open to pursuing it.

We have our work cut out for us, but honestly, the only thing I care about right now is getting home to Marcy. The pain and fury etched on her beautiful face haunt me. I won't rest until she's safe in my arms again.

She's the only thing that matters to me, and I'll be damned if I let anyone else hurt her. I'll rip the city apart if it ensures her protection.

I love her. And nothing will ever keep us apart.

Chapter Twenty-Five
Marcy

"What the hell happened to you?" I rush across the room when Rob walks in the door. The right side of his face is swollen, and a dark purple shiner is forming around his eye. He winces when I cup his cheek to inspect the damage.

"Had a run-in with Vic Simmons at the lawyer's."

Bile bites the back of my throat at the mention of that name. "Did you hit him first?"

"Yes." He grins.

"That was stupid. Now he'll come after you."

"I'd like to see him try." He kisses my forehead. "I'm sorry he hurt you, baby."

My heart pounds at the sweet gesture. "Sit down here." I motion to the couch, then grab a bag of frozen veggies from the freezer and wrap them in a tea towel. "Here, put this on it."

He presses the bag gingerly to the side of his face, focusing on me with his good eye. "Thanks."

"I hope he walked away with one to match." I gesture to his face.

"Better." Rob grins like he won the lottery. "I broke the bastard's nose."

A gasp rips from my throat even as pride fills me. "You didn't?"

"I did." His grin fades to a self-satisfied smirk. "Caught him off guard too." Rob flexes his right hand. "I think I fractured my metacarpals though."

"Your what?"

"The bones in my hand." He chuckles. "I think they're broken."

I shake my head. "You're a mess."

"Yeah, but I'm your mess now." He pulls me close and

presses a soft kiss to my lips.

My heart warms at the action. "You're lucky I love you."

"Luckiest man alive." He flinches at the uncomfortable position.

Pulling back, I settle beside him and study his handsome face. "So what happened after I left? The lawyer didn't seem too convinced we could win. Then Vic's team showed up and offered a deal to keep it all quiet."

"They're trying to reach an agreement so we don't take it to court."

"Did the lawyer say we should take a deal?"

Rob exhales sharply, the sound of exhaustion echoing through the room. "At first, that's exactly what he thought we should do. Then I offered some deeper insight into the charming Vic Simmons's history."

I nudge him with my elbow. "The suspense is killing me. Out with it."

"Richards did some digging and found some unflattering records on Simmons. Old charges that were dismissed out of court. Probably paid off to keep their mouths shut."

"How does that help me?" I pout at the disappointing revelation. "If he's gotten away with this before, there's no way in hell we'll get him this time."

"Not necessarily." Rob lowers the ice pack and holds my gaze. "It establishes he has a history of this type of behavior. If we can find other women he's assaulted, we might be able to throw a wider net. Plus, we have a witness who's willing to testify on your behalf. That counts for something."

"How are we going to find other victims? He travels extensively, and no one is going to want to air that kind of dirty laundry." I bite the edge of my nail in a lame attempt to quell my rising anxiety.

"Richards is calling in a few favors. I'm sure he left a trail. Trust me"—Rob's face softens—"he won't get away with this, baby. I promise."

"I do trust you." I take his hand and kiss the reddened knuckles before placing the ice-cold bag on them. "But I can't just sit here and do nothing."

"Maybe it's time we took your story public."

The suggestion leaves me off-kilter.

"If you step forward, maybe it'll encourage others to do the same."

Fear lodges in my throat, choking me. Unwelcome memories flood me, and I pinch my eyes closed.

You're safe. You're safe. Breathe.

"Breathe, Marcy. Just breathe."

When I open my eyes, Rob's kind eyes are filled with compassion. "There you go. In. Out. In. Out. Breathe, baby."

Slowly the panic subsides, and I'm able to focus again. "I don't know if I can."

"I won't force you. This is your decision." He licks his lips. "But if you take your story public, I guarantee others will come forward."

"Who would run a story like that? Simmons's powerful and popular and influential. No media outlet in their right mind would run the story."

"They might if they were granted first rights to any information pertaining to the case and exclusive interviews."

"You want me to parade myself in front of the press?"

Rob's eyes darken two shades. "No. I don't. I want to protect you as much as I can from these vultures." He sighs. "But the truth is, if this goes to court, they're going to start digging regardless, and it would be better for us to stay out in front of it."

"Fuck." My head droops.

Rob hooks his finger under my chin and lifts my gaze. "I have faith in you. Whatever happens, we'll do this together."

Tears prick my eyes. "What if it's all for nothing and he gets away with it?"

"Could you live with the regret if you don't follow through?"

I shake my head vehemently. "No, especially if he hurts someone else and I could have stopped him." A sob sticks in my throat. "I can't let that happen. Not while there's a breath in my body."

"I didn't think so." He wraps his arm around me and pulls me against his solid chest. "You have support. Me. Arthur and Kate. Donna and Liana. We're all right here with you, all the way."

Even though I'm not at peace with the decision, confidence infiltrates every fiber of my being. "Thank you."

He kisses my forehead. "For what, baby?"

I lean back to meet his gaze. "For loving me even though I'm a beautiful disaster."

"You're beautiful without a doubt, and this is quite a disaster. But that doesn't mean you're broken in any way." He brushes a lock of hair away from my face. "I love you regardless."

Our lips meet in a sweet kiss. My hunger for him soon overwhelms my sense. I climb into his lap and cradle his face in my hands, deepening the kiss. My touch is gentle, aware of the bruising.

Rob grasps my hip with his left hand, gently pressing my thigh with his injured right one. He hisses against my lips.

I pull away, but he hooks his arm around my waist and holds me still.

"I don't want to hurt you."

"I'll be fine," he murmurs against my cheek. "I need you just like this."

When I search his eyes for a flicker of pain, I'm lost. This sweet, compassionate, wonderful man…how have I lived this long without him? And how can I ensure I never have to be parted from him for a moment longer? "I love you, Rob."

"I love you too." He nuzzles against my neck. "We'll get through this together."

"Then what?" I gasp when he kisses the sensitive spot below my ear.

"Guess we'll figure that out when we get there."

"Will you marry me?"

The moment the words leave my lips, the weight of them dissipates into the air.

"Wait. What did you say?" Rob grips my shoulders and

holds my gaze. "Say it again."

"Marry me, Rob."

"Are you feeling okay?" He presses the back of his hand to my forehead. "Are you feverish? Delusional?"

I laugh and shake my head. "No. I'm serious."

"Oh, thank God, I thought I was imagining things for a moment." His smile turns effervescent. "Is that what you want?"

"Absolutely."

"You're sure?"

"Positive."

He sighs in relief. "Good, because I'm getting too old for this waiting-around bullshit."

I roll my eyes. "Don't be so dramatic."

"I wasn't being dramatic. I was just waiting for the woman of my dreams to realize I've wanted her for years."

My hand rests on his heart. "Why didn't you say something sooner?"

"Trying to convince her of anything is like walking on broken glass."

"Totally dramatic." I chuckle. "So what's your answer?"

"Yes." He kisses me softly. "I will marry you, Marcy."

Elation consumes me. Together we fall in a mass of tangled limbs and murmured groans, dinner forgotten. After the first two orgasms, I stop counting and enjoy the bliss of finally securing the love of my life. Neither of us can fight this feeling anymore, and for once, I surrender willingly.

We have a long road ahead of us, but together we can conquer anything life throws our way.

CHAPTER TWENTY-SIX
ROB

A Year Later...

"In the case of Vic Simmons, we the jury find the defendant guilty on all counts."

A round of applause shakes the courthouse. Marcy visibly relaxes when the verdict is read. I wrap my arms around her.

"It's over, baby. We got him."

"Finally." She buries her face against my chest.

On the other side of the room, Kate and Arthur beam with pride.

Six months of interviews and testimony gave us all the ammunition we needed against the bastard. When Marcy's story hit the stands, a flurry of calls came in. With Richards's connections, we were able to put together a case against Simmons. He tried to settle, but the allegations kept piling up until he couldn't hide any longer. It went to court.

And we won the suit against him.

Later that night, we gather at Arthur's penthouse to celebrate.

"You should be proud, Marcy." Arthur offers his congratulations. "He'll finally get what he deserves."

"Even better than that, he'll think twice before trying that shit with another woman now that he's been branded an abuser." Kate hugs Marcy. "I can't believe the number of women who came forward with their stories."

"Your bravery gave them courage." Arthur pours another glass of tea from the pitcher on the table. "I'm extremely proud of you for standing up and speaking out against him, even though it put you in an awkward position."

"Airing your own dirty laundry for all the world to see isn't easy, but you did it." Kate takes Marcy's hand.

"It wasn't easy, but I'm glad I did it." Her gaze turns to me. "I couldn't have done what I did without you by my side." She leans back against me.

I wrap my arm around her waist. "I told you. We're with you until the end, baby."

"What'll happen now?" she asks.

"Jail time. Restitution." I shrug. "We have to wait until sentencing."

"They don't castrate them?" Marcy jokes, half-serious.

"I wish," Kate murmurs.

"So it's still a problem in the future, huh?" Arthur rests his arm on his wife's shoulder.

"Yes. I wish I could say it gets better, but it doesn't."

I hold Marcy tighter.

"So what's next for you two?" Kate changes the subject.

"We have an appointment next week in upstate New York to look at a house." Marcy's excitement is infectious. "Rob's taking a job there as the local doc."

"That's wonderful. You both deserve a break after the last year." Kate claps her hands together.

Marcy wiggles against me. It was difficult for both of us, putting ourselves in front of the cameras and exposing her difficult history. We fought hard trying to protect ourselves, but in the end, she took a hiatus from her job when the story broke and the press went wild. Liana and Donna took over the business, leaving Marcy to indulge in her other passions—namely me.

It didn't stop her from helping other women find their voices and their freedom. Claude thanks her every day for helping Gwen last winter. I'll miss seeing them together at the Black Penny every week.

When she found the perfect location to open a cute boutique upstate, that sealed the deal. I put in my notice at the hospital last month. It's time for a change. As much as we both love the city, we're ready for a new adventure. Together.

"The boutique will be just up the road from Rob's office."

She glances at me with an infectious grin before returning her attention to her brother and Kate. "You'll come visit, right?"

"You won't be able to keep us away." Kate leans against Arthur. "We'll be looking for a new place soon. There's no room here for a baby."

"Baby?" Marcy jumps up, wrenching herself from my arms. "You're pregnant?"

Kate nods. "I just found out."

"Congratulations." I offer felicitations to my best friend and his time-traveling bride. "I'm so happy for the both of you."

Marcy and Kate hug, falling into chatter about their plans and possible names. I stand and stretch my legs, walking to the window overlooking the city. Arthur comes alongside me.

"You're going to be a father. How does that make you feel?" I clap my hand on his shoulder.

"Terrified." He grins, and there's a sparkle of joy in his eyes. "But I wouldn't have it any other way."

"I'm so excited for both of you." I chuckle. "As improbable as it is, you knocking Kate out with a door is the best thing that has ever happened to you."

"Yeah. There are days I wonder if she's really here…if she's real."

"She's real, and after watching *Back to the Future* last year, I can't say I'd completely discount time travel as real."

Arthur snorts. "She didn't come here in a DeLorean."

"No, but there's a lot of shit we can't explain in the universe."

"Maybe I'll just chalk it up to fate."

I laugh. "Fate, huh? Listen to you. Never thought I'd hear you say something like that, Mr. Practicality."

"I'm too old to fight it."

"Yeah, me too." I look out over the city as the sun sets in the west, setting the buildings alight with bursts of orange and red.

"So where are you planning on moving?"

"Not sure yet. We have a few months to figure it out. But I'm sure we'll stay in the city."

"Any word from your driver, Cyril?"

"Not since Christmas." Arthur leans against the window. "I've put all his stuff in storage at the garage."

"What are you going to do with it?"

"What he would have wanted. If he shows up, it's his. If not, well…"

The implication of the words settles between us, weighed down with regret.

"He'll show up. You'll see."

"I hope so." Arthur shakes his head and straightens. "How about we go out for dinner? My treat. Today is a day for celebrations."

Kate's head snaps up. "Can we go to the diner? I've been craving apple pie and vanilla ice cream."

We all laugh, and the sound soothes like a healing balm.

"We'll stop for dessert, I promise." He retrieves her purse from the table.

"Shall we?" I offer Marcy my arm, and she takes it, fitting her hand in the crook of my elbow like it was always meant to be there.

This moment was a long time coming, but it was well worth the trials along the way. Contentment settles over me.

I finally have the woman of my dreams, and she has my heart. Forever.

I can't fight this feeling anymore, and I wouldn't have it any other way.

THE END

Hello, again, dear Reader,

Thank you for reading Marcy and Rob's story, *Can't Fight This Feeling*. I hope you enjoyed their emotional and rewarding journey. I know I enjoyed writing it.

I never intended to make this a series, but when I met Rob and Marcy in *When I Found You,* I was compelled to write their story as well as stories for Detective Richards, Claude, and Cyril. Their stories will be coming soon.

If you found any parts that weren't accurately portrayed, I apologize. My resources and research only led me so far when it came to legal, medical, and architectural details. I'm not a professional stylist, nor do I personally know one, so I had a little fun filling in those blanks. Again, my apologies if there were any inconsistencies or inaccuracies, I did my best to write a historically feasible story.

This also goes for any slang that may have been a year or two off. It was so difficult to stick to the first half of the 80s when there were so many great pop culture references and slang from the second half.

As for the court case against Vic Simmons, well, I know these kinds of sexual assault cases rarely made it to court in the 1980s and even more rarely were those suits successful. They are more of a modern trend starting in the 1990s. However, New York State had laws on the books as early as 1965 concerning sexual assault, making the premise plausible.

Thank you again for reading and I hope you'll continue with the series. I have lots of drama and romance in store for the remaining three books.

Sincerely,

Kirsten S. Blacketer

Other Books by Kirsten S. Blacketer

Craving 1985 Series
When I Found You
Can't Fight This Feeling
She Gives Love a Bad Name
Owner of a Lonely Heart
Just What I Needed

Historical
An Irresistible Shadow
A Shadow's Kiss
Mississippi Moonshine
Deceiving the Earl
Jewel of Winter
At Winter's Demand
Under Winter's Control
Seducing Winter's Gentleman
Stealing the Widow's Heart
Seduction on the Alpine Express
Temptation on the Alpine Express

Contemporary
A Lockdown Love Affair
A Holiday Love Affair
Mistletoe and Mistakes
Confessions of a Fangirl
Confessions of a Gamer Girl
Confessions of a Glamour Girl
The Flight Before Christmas

Fantasy/FairyTale
Curse of the Huntsman's Jewel
The Huntsman's Revenge

Pirates and Persuasion
Queen Takes Hook

ABOUT THE AUTHOR

Kirsten S. Blacketer is a multi-published indie author of both historical and contemporary romance. When she's not writing, she homeschools her two children and enjoys time with her family. In those moments of freedom, she devours romance novels while sipping a glass of wine. Age has only shown her that writing villains can be just as fun as heroes. Her next life goals are to write a New York Times Bestseller and one day have Adam Driver play a starring role in a film version of one of her books. A girl can dream, right?

Read more at **http://kirstensblacketer.com.**

ALSO WRITES AS JEN BRADLEE